CHINELO

CHINELO

By
Okafor Mansim

Fourth Dimension Publishing Co., Ltd.

First Published 1985 by
FOURTH DIMENSION PUBLISHING CO., LTD
16 Fifth Avenue, City Layout. PMB. 01164, Enugu, Nigeria.
Tel+234-42-459969. Fax+234-42-456904.
email: fdpbooks@aol.com, fdpbooks@yahoo.com
Web site: http://www.fdpbooks.com.

Reprinted 2002

ISBN 978-156-194-7

Photoset and printed in Nigeria by
Fourth Dimension Publishers, Enugu.

CHINELO

Dedicated to my mother, Madam Ojiugo Florence Okafor, a firm rock of a woman who, though frail with hardships, pains and worries, perservered in absolute silence to the end.

This is the product of that perseverance,
Not mine but yours through, my forebearance,
This is the fulfilment of that covenant,
As by traditional ordinance,
For I do remember my promise,
Just before his demise,
To show the light,
That will send darkness to flight,
You must have seen the rays
Showing smiling faces all the way
I have, as always, kept my word
Leaving you to see and also, the world.

Your third child
Your second son,

OBIDIGBO.

"Uzoh," Mazi Egwuonwu called out when he was through with his dinner. "No, Nkem," he corrected himself just before Uzoh could answer his call. "Come and take away these plates," he regally directed as he had always done.

"When it comes to setting up the meals, I'm called but when it comes to clearing up, they look for their favourites," Uzoh murmured and sulked in her corner.

"That is the life of a woman, my daughter but I've always told you that you are presently too big to be fighting your juniors over food remains," chipped in Chinwude, Uzoh's Mother.

"If I'm too big to quarrel over food remains then I'm equally too big to serve food," Uzoh argued and refused to be intimidated. "And from today, I'll just do the cooking any other person could do the serving."

"Don't let your father hear that," Chinwude advised her daughter more politely when she discovered that she had lost the argument. "Nkem, take that soup bowl to the kitchen so that more soup should be added to it to do you three's meal tonight. I don't have to cook soup everyday in this house," Chinwude complained more to forge a compromise with her daughter, then to chide anybody.

Uzoh felt happy that neither she nor Nkem had won the covetted bowl of soup. Nkem fumed like concentrated sulphuric acid as he looked at the three pieces of dry fish in the bowl and then at the direction of his mother. He gruntled in an unidentified foreign language which only he ι knew as he walked heavily towards the kitchen, when it dawned on him that he had lost a major battle for possession.

"Stop breaking up the floor of the house with your sole just for a few pieces of fish. It's no use; whether you cry or laugh, just do as I've said, Usa," Chinwude cursed.

Nkem hated being called a greedy "long throat" over what he considered his divine right as the most favoured child, the only son.

1

But whatever the name they called him, he cared not but insisted on claiming his right, if not all his right, some, if not legally, illegally, if not in the open, clandestinely but immediately.

As he moved towards the kitchen, he quickly counted the main pieces of fish in the soup bowl and they were three. He balanced the soup bowl precariously on his left hand and with the right, fished out the largest piece into his ready mouth. That was before Uzoh remembered to shadow him. Both of them entered the kitchen together with Uzoh not learning much from the inactivity of Nkem's mouth. Within, it bubbled with the activity of a sleeping volcano.

Uzoh counted the pieces of fish as she poured in the extra soup. She found two and because, she wasn't aware of the original number, she hadn't any cause for suspicion more so, when Nkem's jaw didn't show any signs of recent activity. She did a good mental division of the two pieces between three people.

"I'll take the smaller one, Nkem and Obiageli will share the other one." She racked her young brain. She didn't foresee any sources of mathematical errors. To her, the division was perfect.

Uzoh, not trusting Nkem with the soup took it herself to their eating spot at one corner of the family's small parlour, Nkem grudgingly picked up behind with the extra amount of pounded cassava foofoo to complement the extra soup.

Uzoh and Obiageli were already seated when Nkem arrived. Both ladies sat with their legs stretched forward straight before them. Obiageli sat behind Uzoh with her two legs touching the outward sides of her small buttocks. There was no space for Nkem at this side of the ring. Instead, there was one in front of Uzoh, behind Obiageli. Uzoh wanted to have a clear view of Nkem while they ate and Nkem was aware of this. He hated the idea and tried desperately to squeeze himself behind Uzoh. He gave up when Uzoh coldly asked him if he was blind. Having lost this important initial battle of wits, he humbly took up his rightful position in front of a victorious Uzoh and sat cross-legged like a Yogi.

When all was set, Uzoh asked that all should close their eyes so that they prayed. They all closed their faces with their palms but only Obiageli actually closed her eyes. Nkem watched Uzoh and the soup plate with one eye from a crevice between two partially separated fingers while Uzoh watched Nkem critically from a similar opening.

Prayers over, each ate silently with Uzoh frequently making small balls for Obiageli to encourage her to eat fast. But Uzoh ate very little herself. She wasted most of her time trying to monitor Nkem's activities as he ate because he was good at pilfering small pieces of fish from the soup. He had a way of doing it without detection no matter the security mounted by Uzoh. But today, security was just too tight as Uzoh plugged all loopholes and waited to see how Nkem could out-wit her again. She made sure they ate at virtually the same rate with Nkem's hand entering the soup bowl just a shade of a second before her hand. Suffice it to add that her eyes followed Nkem's right hand wherever it went. Her close scrutiny brought order to their feeding and there was peace.

While they ate, their father shook his two legs to fight the soporific effect of the heavy food as he relaxed on the verandah. He belched loudly, and then remembered that Mazi Okwumah had just brought in the evening's collection of palm wine.

Mazi Okwumah was the palm wine tapper who really knew his trade. No one ever tasted his wine and asked for another, not even the Oyibo wine. He tapped for Mazi Egwuonwu and each took the yield on alternate days. He collects his wine twice daily. The evening yield was supposed to be kept to supplement the next mornings yield. But most people seldom resist the temptation to have a few cups. No, not of Okwumah's wine, the temptation was always too great. Mazi Egwuonwu wasn't an exception. He didn't resist the temptation long before he gave in.

He went into his pitch-dark room and soon came out with the calabash keg of palm wine and his drinking bull horn. He balanced the keg between his legs and dusted the bull-horn's interior with his hand. Not satisfied, he blew into it twice and without much ado, filled it to the brim with the white frothing liquid from the keg balanced on his left knee. He emptied the contents of the horn in a gulp, belched again and shook his head from side to side.

"Tufia," he coursed. "This man does not tap palm wine any longer. What he produces with his hand now is nothing but Wikisi (whisky). You wouldn't kill me with your style of tapping coo," he said as he refilled his cup.

"But the wine still tastes like young wine even though the palm trees are twelve year olds. Maybe, he didn't wash his gourds," he argued with himself or with the horn-full of palm wine. "It is nobody's fault," he finally concluded as he gulped half of the horn, "the poor man has too many things to think of."

"Did you call me," Chinwude his wife asked as he was about to pack the keg and drinking horn inside.

"I did not call you, woman," he promptly answered rudely. "But as you have met me well, you could as well come and have a cup," he added as an after-thought.

Chinwude received the cup-full of palm wine with two hands, and knelt down on one knee as she drank the palm wine. When the contents were about three quarters down, she handed the remains back to her husband with two hands.

"Finish it, good woman," he teased her, "Your kindness flows like a stream. You are not able to finish a cup now but when you people go to your useless meetings, you finish a gallon and chew the container."

"And you men don't," she countered.

"Drink and give me my cup," he hollered at her in feigned aggression, "Whenever there are edibles you women start answering ghost calls but come work, you develop faulty ears and start hearing with difficulty."

"I hope you'll be able to sleep tonight for giving me a watery cup of tasteless palm wine," she pulled his legs.

"Women? Only good at talking. Anyone that judges you by what you say will not rest until he has killed all of you. Never mind, the tortoise said that some other fellow will die and there'll be another funeral."

Mazi Egwuonwu refilled his drinking horn and emptied the contents into his mouth to help digest the joke he had just cracked with his wife when the alarm sounded.

"I've now come to accept the fact that it is a luxury for me and my wife to have rest and peace in this house," he complained. "Uzoh and Nkem, come here instantly."

The crying immediately ceased and in no time, two fuming faces appeared at the door way each breathing heavily like one who pounded a large mortar of cassava foofoo.

* * * * * *

Uzoh never swallowed a lump of foofoo except she was sure that the contents of the soup bowl were safe within the interval. This took much of her time and attention that she ate very little. Even the little she ate was with much difficulty. As she cautiously took one of her small balls, the mischievous. thing refused to go down her throat. She had not concentrated on it, so it had refused to obey the normal laws of involuntary action. She choked and beat her hands and legs frantically for air which was not readily forthcoming.

"Water, Water," she yelled at Nkem who looked on with pity and quickly handed her the cup of water.

She drank with relish with the cup covering her blazing tear-filled eyes. Obiageli was at the point of breaking down.

"Sorry, sorry sorry . . .," she sang on until Uzoh found her voice to answer. Nkem had greeted her previously but was ignored either deliberated or otherwise.

When she was fully relieved, Uzoh instantly resumed her hobby only to learn much to her surprise that the smaller of the two pieces of fish had disappeared mysteriously. She didn't know whom to suspect, Nkem whom she had been watching very critically for the past moment or the little Obiegeli whom she never cared to shadow. After a very brief consideration, she cast her net on Nkem. But it hadn't been long since she slackened her guard on him in which case, he wouldn't have finished chewing the fish. He wouldn't be able to swallow it whole. So, the piece of fish must still be in Nkem's mouth which she watched very critically. Nkem was aware of her intense gaze and wanted to protest but wouldn't bear to open his mouth. He instead preferred to keep his jaws tightly at bay and tried to break up the solid in his mouth with his tongue but with little success.

Uzoh noticed the nearly imperceptible movement of Nkem's mouth and waited for the catch. Nkem could bear any pains than be caught stealing a piece of fish. So, he decided to swallow it whole.

He made a large family sized ball of foofoo, dabbed it generously with the Egusi soup, brazed up and swallowed hoping to push the fish down with the coloured ball. Half way down, he lost his courage and the ball/fish alliance reflected this change in policy. The ball/fish complex made a U-turn just at the junction of his throat and his mouth. And before he could restrict it, he involuntarily threw out. The evidence as to who ate the runner bean became visibly apparent on the faeces; the piece of fish was firmly embedded inside the ball of foofoo.

Uzoh was enraged but Nkem ignored her as he busied himself drinking water. He drank slowly to gain time but Uzoh wasn't amused. When he couldn't show his face, quick enough, she resisted a strong urge to slap the cup off his shaky hands. She did the alternative by landing the big ball she was having on his right shoulder. She nearly knocked the cup down.

Nkem jumped up like a cat grabbing a hand full of foofoo as he went. He took aim with his right hand. He piloted the ball wrongly with one of his left hand fingers and the ball landed meters away from agile Uzoh. Nkem who hadn't scored a solid hit was busy retrieving a patch from the wall when a solid one landed on one side of his face. That was more than he could bear. He knew he was losing the battle and needed a *coup-de-grace* to place him at par with Uzoh. He thought fast and got the answer.

Nkem charged Uzoh with the fury of a mad cow. Uzoh thought he was coming for physical combat and ran out towards the back yard to have room enough to deal with him. Though their father had banned fighting during meals, she had no alternative than to resort to it if only to bring Nkem down to size. More so, as Nkem started the fight himself.

But Nkem had no plans of starting a physical fight he was sure to lose. He instead preferred a brain war he could conveniently win.

As Uzoh ran out and waited to ambush Nkem, he changed his direction and instead made for the bowl of soup. Uzoh waited in vain for Nkem to appear. She had started wondering what that mischievous bag of tricks was up to when Obiageli's sharp cry awakened her to the realities of what might have happened inside the parlour. She dashed in to discover that the other piece of fish was gone.

"You must vomit it, you thief," she insisted as she held Nkem's throat and tried to choke him into submission.

Nkem tried desperately to ignore the threat of assassination. He reluctantly gave in when she showed no signs of relenting her squeeze and out came all the contents of his mouth.

"That is for being too daring," she said thereafter, slapping him in the process.

Nkem, who was still recovering from two choking attempts yelled out at the unexpected but perfect attack.

"I've died, I've died," was all Mazi Egwuonwu and his wife, Chinwude, could hear to know that Uzoh and Nkem had once more disagreed over pieces of fish.

* * * * * *

"It is now routine that any time I provide food for you in this house, I provide a source of discontent. But I am happy that you didn't quarrel for lack of foofoo or soup but over pieces of fish. It now seems as if such condiments serve no useful purpose for both of you except as fuel for a fight. I've instructed my wife not to add meat or fish into your soup but she wouldn't have it. I've spoken until my lips have all peeled off. I wonder whom you resemble in this behaviour. Surely not my humble self or your good mother who could give my lunch away to anybody in need. I've thought over it for a time now and it seems as if children don't resemble either of their parents any longer. What do you want me to say when children who sucked the same breast couldn't see eye to eye with each other. In our own time, brothers and sisters don't treat each other like this instead they protect one another. Our forefathers didn't behave like this either. They loved one another. They were their brothers' keepers. They never. . ."

Mazi Egwuonwu suddenly stopped in mid-sentence and his countenance changed. He looked sad and disturbed. He suddenly aged. A thought had occurred to him on his forefather's behaviours. To verify his thought, he suddenly turned his right hand and there was the black tumour-like birth mark that resembled a small sixth finger attached to the last little finger.

Chinwude, Uzoh and Nkem watched on in wild bewilderment as his right hand flew back to his left shoulder as if he had been stung by a wasp. His right hand felt the big scar which excited him on being touched.

The two brought back a painful memory of one aspect of life by his forefathers that wasn't worth boasting about; it wasn't good remembering. It brought bitter memories of yesteryears. So, he shook his head to remove the sad memory but it was indelible.

"Go away." He finally said to his confused children. "A frequently repeated message makes the mouth feel sour. Try and treat each other well as brothers and sisters would. Uzoh, try and show a little maturity. Treat your younger brother as your son. Nkem, respect Uzoh as a senior and avoid your tendency of being too greedy. Only in love and togetherness do we gain. No one gains anything in malice and quarrels. Uzoh, go and get another piece of fish and share. I don't want to hear any noise from that end."

When they had left, Mazi Egwuonwu remained silent for quite a period. His wife watched unobserved as she tried to figure out what had caused her husband's bizzare behaviours.

"You are germinated seedlings of true seeds of your forefathers. You were not budded or grafted but true sons and daughters of your forefathers. It may not be your fault after all but it's unfortunate that children should take after the bad characters of their parents and leave the good ones. It is in the blood, right within the blood; blood doesn't tell lies."

"What happened to her?" he softly asked the eternal darkness that had engulfed both his body and mind. "Was she kidnapped?" he continued to ask without receiving the answer to his first question. "Did the god of the people take her as a punishment for trying to humiliate it? Or was she taken by the goddess of the river to end her suffering? What really happened to my sister I loved with all my heart?" he asked with tears in his eyes. As always, when he failed to find an answer, he waved his two open hands as a sign of frustration. He waved as he and others had done eighteen years ago. And with that, the mystery of what really happened to Chinelo remained as dark and tightly covered as the day he had come back from the River of Seven Spirits with Agubamba and the basket of cloths but without the owner of the cloths.

"What really happened to her?" he asked once more.

The answer remained the same. He opened his hand in frustration.

Thereafter, he relapsed into deep silence as he tried to recollect as far as he knew. He tried to recollect the story of a dazzling beauty from the good sweet beginning to the revulsive bitter end. He shuddered at the agonising story but remained as mystified as he was eighteen years ago.

"What happened to Chinelo?" he asked with a trembling voice as tears fell freely.

The dark night failed to present an answer. Egwuonwu opened and waved his hand in frustration once more as he and others did very long ago.

* * * * * *

Unaku's hand groped slowly in the darkness of the room as it made its way towards Nnenna's sleeping position. She could see her outline very clearly, from the reflecting flicker of log fire supplied benevolently by two pieces of dry palm trunks. Though she was very apparent on the earth-raised bed/seat, her mother took her time so as not to jostle her violently which could drive off her soul with the resultant death.

"Nnenna," she called out softly even before her hand got to her. "My grandmother," she continued when her hand found her stomach. Unaku moved her hand down to her legs and tapped them softly to arouse her while still calling her name as softly as she could.

"I've always said that you children are very strong. How couldn't one be so tired after running around virtually all the night? " Unaku asked in praise of the strength of youth. "I pity you and would have allowed you to sleep on except that we have no single drop of drinking water," she tried to justify her action.

"Who told you we have no drinking water?" Nnenna asked right and clear in a voice which indicated she had been clowning being asleep. "We went to the spring yesternight after the moon play. But I still want to go. I forgot to wash some of my dresses."

"Tortoise," Unaku labelled her, "so, you've been awake all this while and yet allowed me to be breaking my head unnecessarily."

"Mother, I feel so lazy to rise and leave this cosy bed for the dry harmattan outside. The heat from this fire has permeated my entire bone marrow and my brain."

"Rise, you lazy drone," she jokingly admonished her, "your mates are waiting for you outside."

The last information was unnecessary because Nnenna had been aware of this from the onset. She had lain still in the hope that she was dreaming but realities seldom turn into dreams. Her mother's information simply confirmed such a reality.

Nnenna gave a very long free yawn, rolled from side to side and on the third count, jumped up.

"I'm coming," she called out to the group outside. "Mother, good morning. I nearly forgot to greet you."

"Good child, have you woken?" she formally asked even though she knew her daughter had (after all, she hadn't been discussing with someone asleep). "I hope you slept well," she continued even though she as well knew that her daughter barely slept throughout the night.

Minutes later, Nnenna discussed merrily down the spring path as the strong harmattan wind took particular care to keep them dry and cold. She had an earthenware pot precariously balanced on a ring made of dry plantain stem and leaves which she had on her head. She felt weak after the night's play in the village's play ground with her age mates. She hated the sickening feeling of weakness but couldn't keep away from plays just because of the hang-overs, after all, the fear of being killed never prevented soldiers from fighting their wars. Even as she went down the steep hill that led to Otta spring, she could still hear the beckoning song calling her out for the night's play:

> Onye aputaro
> Elim utala elilisie ya isi, elim utala,
> Onye aputaro,
> Elim utala elilisie ya isi, elim utala,
> Nnenna aputaro
> Elim utala elilisie ya isi, elim utala. . . . .

Ijeomah sang while a host of other children chorused. Any new arrival lent more force to the chorusing intensity. Even those smaller children not in her play group enjoyed the privilege of singing with them.

Nnenna had recently observed a certain sequence in calling the names of those who hadn't turned up for the night's play. Her name usually came up last in the roll call and immediately her name was called, Ijeomah seemed to forget that any other name existed. She would repeat her (Nnenna's) name until she showed up. In addition, many people had recently taken up more liking for her. Virtually, all the mature boys in their group hussled to team up with her in most competition. In the hide and seek game, which she loved very much, the boys literally squeezed life out of each other as they crowd together around her in her preferred hiding place. This frequently attracted the attention of the seekers. She more often than not, got caught while the more clever boys easily found their ways to safety. Nnenna found it very difficult to explain this new surge in interest. It may, however, not be unconnected with the fact that, since the exit of Ekenma who got married, she had become the next eligible bride. More still, she was not ugly.

A lot of people were already at the spring when they arrived. While one of her cousins helped her collect water in her pot, Nnenna rushed down to the adjacent Kisa stream to do her laundry. She came back on time to join the other females at the female bathing section. The males went to the opposite bathing area.

Despite the harmattan, the spring was still very warm. But Nnenna tensed all the same as she approached the water sprout that sent several jets of water down from a height of about three meters. She was still doing the count down amidst a deafening chorus by well concealed toads and frogs when a gentle hand suddenly nudged her into the path of a warm jet of water. She screamed involuntarily only to welcome the warm water that boldly caressed her skin around the face and chest. Slightly warmer quantities of water ran down the whole length of her body to her feet.

"Who committed this abominable crime?" Nnenna asked when she found her breath.

"My *asa* who baths just for the sake of doing so having been divinely bathed by her creator," Ogonna, her newly married aunt flattered her. "I've always said that you can't ascape my senior brother in marriage. As your uncle swam seven seas to come and marry me, so will my brother do in revenge."

"My father's wife," Nnenna said in a mock show of resentment, "if there is anything you want to tell me this morning better say it but stop teasing me."

"I now believe on what the dog said that those who have good buttocks seldom know how to sit well. I wish I were you and I'll have all these men crawling under my feet."

"This woman, what did I do to you this morning to incur your anger? Why have you simply refused me peace this morning?" Nnenna protested to the crowd's amusement.

Nnenna actually enjoyed the flattery and was unaware of the envy of some other girls who covetously admired her exceptional beauty. They watched her bath but some resisted a strong urge to strangle her when she vainly cupped one breast after the other with her right palm. She was ignorant of the time lapse until Ogonna, who had done with her own bathing long ago voiced their impatience.

"My brother's wife, we are still waiting," she said politely. "There is no need of your wasting our time when God has already done all that is necessary. If it were uglies like me, it would have been understandable."

"Eh! I'm coming. But my father's wife, I wonder whether you dreamt of me yesternight that you have decided to kill me with your sarcasm."

They were half way towards home when they saw signs that there was a deadly snake in the house's thatched roof; all the able bodied men of their village were moving, one after the other, in the opposite direction. Many of them appeared briefly on the track road but generally preferred the security of the bush from which they periodically appeared and to which they unfailingly headed for. Repeated inquiry from successive absconders met with indeliberate rebuff as each new arrival disappeared with the speed with which he appeared.

"They can only get the money from my dead body. I have not seen the one with which to eat three square meals a day let alone an extra to give to some other person either for his pocket or that of the government," they heard a voice complaining in the bush as its owner traced the bearing towards the thickest part of the forest. The information didn't help much because they didn't know the source or the people they were running away from. Their nerves were shaking violently around the yield point and their legs were wobbling by the time they negotiated the sharp bend that led to the road junction. There at the road junction, were the terrors, the tax collectors, the rate collectors and a powerful team from the bicycle licencing office of the Divisional Headquarters at Guru. Around them were a few dozens of bicycles they had impounded and even a greater number of dejected men many of whom were busy over the thought of how to battle with the weevil-infested beans and the bed bugs of the Guru prison; a battle no one has ever won.

"Our daughter," called out one of the arrested men, "kindly give me a cup of water so that I may have something in my stomach before they take us to anywhere that pleases them."

Nnenna pitied the old labourer who, even though he paid his tax and water rate, had a bicycle whose license had been last changed in the last six years. The bicycle itself was so old that the arrears of the licensing fee was far more than the cost of the bicycle itself.

"Father, but I have no cup," Nnenna pitifully complained.

"I have one," said the old culprit, Mazi Ugolo, as he fished out an empty sardine can that served as his water cup.

"Father, what did they say you did?" Nnenna ventured to inquire as the old man gulped down a second cup of water.

"Go away with your dirty water," a hostile voice said behind her. "If your inquiry earns you the head of a dog, what do you do with the jaw?"

"Oh, I'm sorry. Don't be annoyed," Nnenna frightfully apologised as she rose with her pot of water which she had knelt down to carry. "I don't know that they should not be spoken to."

The head of the squad was struck dumb by what he heard and saw He didn't know whether it was her beautiful voice or polite manners that made his heart beat like the village talking drum. The total effect of the three made him develop light brain, his head reeled seriously even though he ate very well that morning before work. The effect was not unusual. It was the typical effect of Nnenna's exceptional beauty. It struck men like lightning and left them half paralysed, half deaf, half dumb but fully stupid.

Nnenna was exceptionally beautiful no matter who did the beholding. In an age when females were taller than men, she was as well taller than most of her sexes. Such an outstanding height would have been complimented by a marked slim figure. On the contrary, Nnenna was not slim but could not be considered as being fat; she was at the borderline, the Euglena of her sex. As if these were not enough, a jet black crown of very long hair honoured her small head. This crown was as long as her shoulders when let loose. But letting it loose was not the fashion in vogue. It was instead plaited by the crafty hands of her friend into a "shakara" hairstyle. It was painful to carry things on such plaited hairdos but females can endure anything both for the vanity of their hair and to prove the domesticity of their sex. The hair and the hairdo were just surpluses for a well sculptured face; the face of a water mermaid. This type of face could only be possessed by an "ogbanje" but Nnenna was neither an "ogbanje" nor a descendant of one: It was a face of small features except the eyes. The eyes were large and bright but the nose, mouth and ears were all small. Hidden within the mouth but frequently exposed by incessant smiles were a fine set of ivory-white teeth. She was frontally gap-toothed between her upper pair of incisors. An equally obvious pair of gaps flanked both sides of her perfectly cone-shaped, sharply-pointed and dog-like canine teeth. 'Hence, her smiles were chronically infectious.

Her entire head and its crown of ebony black hair were borne on a delicate yam tendril-like, slender neck. Her victims develop severe symptoms of optical abberation on beholding her face. That could explain their inability to observe her well-formed chest elevations and behinds. That could as well explain the non-observation of her solid limbs, otherwise, it would have been observed that her limbs were thickly covered with a layer of hair. Whether this extended to all parts of her body, no man could know. But her fellow female bathers at the Otta spring were aware of the uncommon extension of her limb hair over her entire body though the tufts were denser in certain parts of the body and less dense in others. It extended from her chest to the ankle via her navel and thigh regions.

But physical appearance, though the most obvious, was not Nnenna's greatest asset. Her most dangerous weapon was her voice; a high-pitched treble which mesmerises virtually everybody when spoken in her characteristic near-whisper, bedroom tone. Then, it sounded like a hundred tiny dwarf bells ringing in the inner chambers of large enclosed cathedral; the sound seemed to come from everywhere and from nowhere in particular. It was a super treble that disarmingly draws the breath and courage of the strong-willed while at the same time having a coquettish tinge that the victim finds difficult to resist. This weapon becomes more devastating when it was used in telling a pathetic folk story and Nnenna was very good at telling such stories. Frequently, she held the entire family spell-bound as she weaved her way gracefully through one story of the tortoise and its wisdom or the other. And an apology tendered, or a request made, with the voice could get even a court Judge to make unrealistic concessions.

Ogbolu became one of the victims of Nnenna's virtues when she apologised for her intrusion.

"Oh!" he exclaimed," is it you? I thought it was one of these unruly village girls," he blurted out as if he knew Nnenna previously. His ignorance was very apparent from the fact that Nnenna was a village girl and not totally innocent of some degree of unruliness.

Nnenna proded herself on the open show of remorse by the head man. She nevertheless continued on her disturbed progress for home.

Ogbolu stood transfixed as Nnenna and her group made for home. He was stunned in disbelief that anything living could be as beautiful. He was still gaping when the old man called him to order.

"She is a very beautiful girl," Mazi Ugolo said to a confused Ogbolu. 'I am an eye witness, even a blind man could see it," Ogbolu humbly accepted. "Do you know her very well?" he asked.

"I only know she is from the Inwelle village but I can easily find out if I want to," the old man baited as he saw a God-sent way of escape.

"Is she married?" Ogbolu continued his inquiry as if he didn't hear the old man say just then that he didn't know the girl well enough.

"I don't think so, otherwise, she won't be tying only one length of wrapper," the old man managed to satisfy him. "Are you looking for a wife?" he politely asked. "Well, give me the contract," he continued when Ogbolu failed to answer his question. To his people, muteness under interrogation was a sign of assent.

"I've never thought of marriage all my life but I think one ought to look responsible sometime in one's life."

* * * * * *

"Do you know how to do it?" her uncle asked her.

She noded in reply.

Nnenna's uncle filled a gourd cup of palm wine and handed it over to Nnenna who bowed as she received it with both hands. Ogbolu smiled from his conspicuous corner.

Nnenna knelt down on one knee, took a mouthful of the strong stuff and as everybody waited in silent anticipation, moved to Ogbolu's corner and handed him the remains. Everybody clapped in acclamation for Nnenna had just wedded Ogbolu by native law and customs. Ogbolu's entourage jubilated for their fortune while Nnenna's friends and relatives rejoiced over theirs. Mazi Ugolo, the go-between, grinned from ear to ear. He had every cause to be glad for he had just fulfilled his own part of an agreement that exempted him from paying tax, water rate and bicycle license for the remaining part of his life.

For some members of Ogbolu's family, Nnenna was a rare fish which only a fortunate one could catch. She captivated every member of the entourage and many entertained some impossible wish that they were Ogbolus.

"I never knew such good things exist in Wamba land," one of them said to the other.

"I never knew someone else saw what I saw," the other replied, "I'll soon form the habit of making friends around here."

"I may not need to do that," the first said, "I'll simply book my name down with our new wife and she'll find one for me."

"I'll block my ears to what our people at home would say if I see one like this," the second Guru man said.

At their own site, friends and relatives of Nnenna climbed over each other to have a glimpse of Ogbolu, the lucky man from the proud Guruland.

"He is the one in the white shoe and red cap," one Inwelian informed the other.

"The good girl married a handsome young man," the other announced. "I was afraid that she would marry a boa constrictor after rejecting the hands of not less than fifteen men in marriage."

"I've always believed that she'll be lucky because our sister was 'well-cooked' and deserves all that is good," replied the second Inwellian.

"Look at his neck, nose, eyes," the other took over, "they even seem to resemble except that she is taller and he fairer in complexion."

The news of Nnenna's marriage wasn't limited to her compound. It was rather wide spread and popular for several reasons. One of them was that Nnenna was a beauty queen who had caused a stir by rejecting not less than fifteen men's hand in marriage among whom were the finest men in the village. Wild rumours of her being a ghost, a python, an "Ogbanje" and even a "man" were frequently heard in the village. Hence, most people didn't expect her to marry at all and were, therefore, surprised when they heard that she would. They were, therefore, more than inquisitive to hear more of the news. More important, however, was the fact that her husband was from Guru.

The people of Guru were Wambas who lived beyond the Great river bank. They, therefore, got in contact with the Oyibos and Edohos early enough to have an edge over the surrounding villages in civilization and education. They were a very proud people who considered the other Wambas inferior and held them in contempt. They frequently deny being Wambas but instead, originated from the East. Nonetheless, they spoke nothing but Wamba albeit, in an adulterated from. Needless to add that they never dreamt of marrying a non-Guru. It was an abomination to do so. It was a condescension on their part and an honour to the non-Guru who saw it as a sign of progress and eventual maturity and culturing of the Guru people.

A related source of joy for the relatives and friends of Nnenna was that her husband was a government worker, the head of the tax collectors. And if there were people who had money during the colonial days, it was the tax collectors. Half of the money they collected went into their pockets and a significant fraction of the remaining went into paying their salaries. They as well received ample gifts such as goats, yams and cockerels from those people they had unofficially exempted from paying tax after invoking powers they didn't have. Their revenue reflected on their cheeks and skin which reflected light like a lady's silver mirror. All adults were aware of the tax collectors fraudulence but nobody seemed to hold it against them. The society seemed blind over their crime but saw only their wealth. Hence, to the people, the only thing of importance about the tax collectors was that they were wealthy. It was, therefore, double blessing that a Guru tax collector had come to marry Nnenna.

Nnenna, her friends and relatives couldn't hold back tears as she was led away into the "pleasure" car that had brought Ogbolu and some of his people. Even her hard-hearted father, Mazi Okwundu, gave an involuntary sigh as his favourite daughter changed ownership.

Half way on her journey to matrimony, her sadness gave way to mixed feelings as the joys of riding in a "pleasure" car took advantage of the vanity of the weaker sex to suppress her sad feeling of being abandoned by a family she so much loved. Her sadness was as well lightened by her anticipation of life at Guru more so, her immediate reception that evening.

The reception she received at Guru was superb. Her beauty, voice and manners won her the approval of those who initially objected to her marriage. Even Ogbolu's senior sister Udego, the leader of the opposition group was captivated and brought into the group of accenters. Ogbolu was very pleased that her sister, the pillar in the decision-making body of the house had at long last given in. He went forward and placed a shilling coin on her face, where she danced, to show his pleasure.

Nnenna embraced all and sundry until her chest became numbed and her joints ached. Yet, she continued for each new arrival, males and females, boys and girls, well and sick, clean and dirty, friends and enemies. By the time she had finished eating pounded yam and fresh fish soup, she could hardly remember that she had relatives and friends back home at Inwelle. Outside the house, co-wives sang her praises.

> Aguba ndi malu mma, nwunye anyi di na ime fa,
> awaliba, mpete malu mma, nwunye anyi di na ime fa,
> Awaliba.
> Aguba ndi nwelu ego, nwanne anyi di na ime fa,
> awaliba, Ogalanya nwelu ego, nwanne anyi di na ime
> fa, awaliba, etc.

These songs of praise from well fed women were frequently interrupted by shouts of:

> Onye Nwe o o! Onye o o!
> Onye Nwe o o! Onye o o!
> Ogbolu nya nwe o o, Ayooo!
> Olili, Olili, Olili, Olili oo,
> Olili biam biam n'onu ka-wuum.

If Nnenna had a way of knowing, similar songs of praise had continued in her father's compound after their departure but this time, in praise of her, her father and mother.

* * * * * *

"Is that our new wife?" one woman asked the other as they passed Ogbolu's house on their way to the Eke daily market.

"You mean the tall black one?" asked the other.

"Yes, the beautiful one."

"Whether beautiful or not, she is still a Wamba, the people who have not seen light. Besides, she is a black centipede."

The other woman kept her peace because she was a church woman who held a different view on ethnicity and other forms of discrimination. In addition, most of her customers were Wambas with whom she had very cordial relationships.

Nnenna wasn't aware of the two women and their discussion. This was because she was bent and totally absorbed in doing the early morning chore which included sweeping the whole compound. She was aided by a bevy of young girls from the family who made sure she swept as little as possible.

Generally, the atmosphere appeared cordial to Nnenna but deep within many Gurus shared the antagonistic view of one of the market women.

With time the absorption of Nnenna into the Guru society was nearly complete. This absorption was hastened when they started learning her other qualities which included story telling and singing. Her sweet voice was quite an asset. Her major short-coming was that she wasn't exceptionally good at farming but Ogbolu had overruled that he had no future intention of establishing a farm plantation. On the contrary, her business acumen which could be traced to her captivating nature was enough for him because Guru had a big daily market which people from both far and near patronised.

Nnenna tasted Guru discrimination when they refused to make her the lead singer in their dancing group even though her voice was the best suited for that purpose. She, however, took it in good faith hoping that their residual antagonism should wear away with time. Unfortunately, it got worse when, after ten years of marriage, Nnenna still didn't have a baby for Ogbolu. Decorum was thrown to the wind and previously latent antagonism turned into open hostility.

Ogbolu was suspended between heaven and earth over the issue. Nnenna was taken to virtually all the native doctors around each of whom said she'll soon put to bed but such optimism faded with time. Finally, Ogbolu's friends and some relatives advised him to take a second wife. He was reluctant initially and was supported by his father though his mother was uncommitted. Despite frequent assurances from her father-in-law and husband, Nnenna lived in hell. She was restless out of the conviction that she owes it as a moral duty to give Ogbolu a child. She hated sharing Ogbolu with any other woman but was prepared to let him have his way if that would make him happy and bring peace.

Then early that morning, when the day was still keeping peoples' faces and identity in serious doubt, Udego arrived.

"I have come," she told a sleepy family which excluded Nnenna who purposely kept away because Udego seldom saw eye to eye with her, "and I have a very important thing to say. There is no need of eyeing me," she addressed Ogbolu. "After saying what I want to say, you can throw me away if you want to."

"Nobody wants to throw you away," corrected her father, in an attempt to diffuse a time bomb, "but greet us first before we hear your message which made you leave your sick husband to die of cold."

"I've greeted all of you together but if that will prevent you from listening to me, then I'll repeat it, Good morning."

"What of your husband and children," Udeze continued to weary out her aggressive mood.

"They are fine," Udego answered reluctantly. "Anything more?" she asked.

When nothing more was forthcoming, she continued.

"I've just come to know if you people have left Ogbolu to die without a child in the name of love?"

"We have," agreed the father.

"Is that so?" she asked her mother.

The poor woman just opened her two hands and grimaced in noncommitment.

"I now believe that she put her charm in the food for all of you to eat. Otherwise, I can't explain this blindness. Ogbolu, what do you say?" she inquired in search of a way of approach.

"The bold brave vulture that rips open the stomach of a corpse, just don't mention my name," came the impolite threatening reply.

"I must continue to call you, the young billy goat that doesn't know its owner. I'll keep on calling you."

"It has come to personal insults," Ogbolu pronounced as he stood up and went outside.

Udego followed him outside to his chagrin. Udeze called his daughter back with little or no success.

"There is no running away from naked realities," she shouted at the top of her voice. "Are you waiting for a time when your age mates daughters have reached marriageable ages before you remarry?" she asked Ogbolu who was listening despite his wish not to. "When I refused your marrying Nnenna, I was over-ruled but now, what I feared have started happening. Yet, this dumb has refused to listen to peoples' good counsel to remarry," she complained at the top of her voice.

Ogbolu left her outside and went back into the house. That was very insulting and it worsened the situation. She increased her volume thereby attracting neighbours.

"Our daughter, what is it this morning," one of the aroused neighbours inquired, "has your husband beaten you?"

"That wouldn't have been a problem. It is this devil my dumb brother married who goes about aborting babies like a sheep," she shouted.

"Lower your voice," the neighbour pleaded unsuccessfully.

"I don't know what she gave to my brother that has made him refuse seeing reason. And when I was talking to him, he walked out on me so that the young sheep his mother bought would keep on bleating," she said as she charged into the house to continue the crusade.

Udeze shook his head as he listened uncomfortably to Udego's wrong approach to a genuine case.

"Who has the cloth being eaten by the goat?" he asked philosophically. "Udego, you can't do this in my house. Carry this your madness back to your husband's home."

"Is that what you said father?" she asked soberly.

"Was I carrying water in my mouth when I spoke to you?" he asked defiantly.

"All right, I'm going," was all she could say as she left very hurt by her father's comments.

Inside the house, Nnenna bemoaned her fate. If only she were pregnant but later aborted as was alleged, she would have been happy as it would prove she was a lady and not a man in disguise. The consolation of Ogbolu and Udeze did little to help her condition. All she wanted was to have a baby which was all that she owed Ogbolu and his family.

Despite Ogbolu's hostility, he saw with his sister that there was a need for a second wife and worse still, time was not on his side. He shared the same opinion with her but hated her guts and noisy attitude. In addition, he didn't want her to glory in his capitulation because, seeing with her would tantamount to accepting his fault in marrying a non-Guru lady.

Not long after his sister's visit, Ogbolu started keeping late nights. With this came repeated information that he had started going in with a young Guru girl. Nnenna was enraged and threatened to pack out of his house but her father-in-law Udeze counselled caution. On the other side, Udego, who had stopped coming to her father's house after the show down, was elated. She eventually made up with Ogbolu to Nnenna's surprise.

Then the news broke that Ogbolu has put his girl friend in the family way and intended to marry her. This was despite the fact that Nnenna had informed him that she felt she was pregnant, a fact that the native doctors confirmed. Ogbolu wouldn't buy that gist any longer because he had heard so much of that news previously only to prove it was a mirage. Ogbolu kept on with his plans and on the marriage day, Nnenna kept away. She sought the comfort of her father's home.

"Don't let that baby abort because your husband is getting married to a second wife," her father told her at a stage when she was looking mad, confused and frustrated. "Just pray that God will let this one stay just to prove to them that they have made a costly mistake in getting a second wife for your husband."

She felt relieved but stayed put in her father's house for two native weeks for the celebrations associated with the marriage to die down. Throughout the period, she knew no peace. The thought of her Ogbolu being locked in a warm embrace with his new wife throughout the night had the inverse effect of keeping her awake most of the night.

During her brief stay at home, Nnenna received all forms of counsel from all and sundry. She listened to all but never accepted all. On the open, she never disagreed with her counsellors but within her, she sifted the grains from the chaff. Among the ones she rejected were those having to do with dissent and confrontation of any type. The best counsel she received was that she should start trade on palm produce. She knew it involved a lot but was prepared to do anything to help keep her away from home and from going insane.

So, immediately on her arrival, she started plans to that effect. With her husband's influence, and her beauty, she had no problems securing a licence and appointment as a produce agent for two foreign companies based in Guru. She started trade instantly with funds from her husband who was doing everything to please her now that he had observed his blunder because she was truly pregnant. Moreover, he wanted to keep the two women apart as much as possible to reduce friction.

Palm oil and kernels were produced in villages around Guru but not in Guru itself, so palm produce agents had to travel to the hinterland to buy the commodities from the villagers including the Inwellians. But because the people of Guru despise the other Wambas, these people could only do business with the Gurus as last resort. Any non-Guru in the trade had a good advantage. Unfortunately, most non-Gurus lack the finance to start such a business. Worse still the Gurus would never allow a non Guru to get near the foreign companies for agent status. So, the produce trade was an exclusive right of Gurus.

Nnenna was between both parties. At Guru, she was a Guru and at Inwelle and other villages, she was an Inwellian and a non-Guru, She, therefore, benefitted both ways being a Guru by marriage and a non-Guru by birth.

With time, Nnenna became a giant in the business having more than twenty carriers. Any time she was absent from market, everyone knew and the market looked like a funeral ground. That was what the market looked like on the third Eke market day after the eclipse. Her ignorant friends and relatives were embarrassed with questions until a close relative brought Ogonna the good news that her sister-in-law had just put to bed that morning.

"What did she get?" Ogonna asked as was customary.

"She gave birth to us," came the reply from the woman.

"Who was that?" a voice asked from behind.

"Nnenna, my sister-in-law, being married at Guru," Ogonna replied.

"Don't bother to explain," the voice advised, "who doesn't know Nnenna, the money woman."

Several other people who overheard the discussion asked for details and in no time, the whole market was alive with the news.

Ogonna hurriedly packed her scanty wares. She bought a large piece of curved dry Asa fish with her little savings and headed home to partake in the jubilation.

That evening, Unaku, Nnenna's mother went down to Guru with a lot of food and other condiments to baby-sit for her daughter and nurse her.

Meanwhile, Ogbolu wasn't finding life easy as his second wife nagged him day-in-day-out when she discovered she hadn't the honour of having the first baby for their husband. Then, when Unaku left, after seven native weeks, the hostility extended to Nnenna who rejoiced over her triumph. She ignored her aggrieved co-wife and watched over her baby very critically. The verbal attack soon turned physical. Though Nnenna could easily beat her mate, she refrained because she could never win a case against a fellow woman heavy with child. Some would even claim that she taunted her mate because she had beaten her to the race of producing their husband's first child. This view was even echoed by her husband during one of their violent quarrels. Nnenna felt so disappointed that she sent a message to her father.

"My daughter does not owe you a penny any longer so, I don't know why she shouldn't have peace in your house. You cannot drive the daughter of Okwundu into a hole she didn't make. And, if anything ever happened to my daughter and her baby, wherever I call you, be prepared to come and answer me there," Mazi Okwundu threatened in a message to Ogbolu.

Ogbolu was frightened to hell after receiving the terse message. He tried to keep the peace until Nnenna was well enough to resume trade personally.

That wasn't long. After the fourteenth native week, Nnenna was back in the market. She received a rousing welcome. She never saw the baby till it was time to feed her as it passed from hand to hand.

Even when the child, named Chinelo, was grown up enough to stop breast feeding, Nnenna still went with her to the market. She couldn't risk keeping her back for her mate, who had put to bed to a baby girl, was capable of any mischief which could make her daughter the first child of the family.

On Eke days at Inwelle, she usually brought her father corn meal with Okoro soup. On such days, she seized the opportunity to find out the family's problems and to bring hers to her stingy father. After such discussion, Nnenna leaves Chinelo behind to play with her cousins while she was away. This soon became a routine practice.

* * * * * *

Mazi Okwundu sat on a stone in front of his hut and busied himself preparing twine ropes with which to tie his yam which had been lying in a heap at one end of his barn. It has been lying there for more than seven native weeks now and the rain was expected anytime from then. He still felt some pains from his waist but had no alternative than to ignore it.

He was expecting his daughter, Nnenna, because, the day was an Eke day, the twentieth Eke of the year. He was, therefore, not surprised when the small children started echoing her arrival.

"Mama Guru has arrived - Oyoyo . . .." they sang as they ran to embrace her.

"My children," she called out at them. "Good children that know their grandmother. I hope you are all well."

"We are," one responded, "but my father flogged me yesterday," he complained.

"I'll ask that wicked man not to flog you again but you must not be heady to your parents and your seniors," she pacified him.

"Ginika slapped me this morning, grandmother," Ngozi complained.

"Don't mind that unmarried mother," Nnenna said to please her even though Ginika was just six years old, "she won't look for her mates but will keep on bullying innocent children who still bathe their stomachs only."

"Grandmother, I washed some bitter leaf in the stream this morning," Ginika said after greeting her aunt. "Do I bring you some to test whether it was well done?"

"My father's mother, I've never spoken of any other person but you. I've always told the Guru people that I don't feel like coming back to them anytime I come here." Nnenna commented proudly as Ginika ran to get her aunt some washed bitterleaf.

The children disappeared mysteriously as Nnenna approached her father. Gone with them was Chinelo who had become so used to her "grandfathers and grandmothers" that she looked forward to every visit.

"Father, how is your waist pains?" Nnenna asked her busy father after they had exchanged routine morning greetings.

"I'm still having them but it is less severe now after the native doctor used his horns to draw out bad blood from that area."

"Sorry. And you must give your body some rest too." Nnenna advised.

"Not when my yams are rotting on the ground and the farming season is approaching."

Nnenna knew the futility of her advice and avoided further persuasion. The father and her daughter discussed both families problems and half way through, Ginika appeared with the bitter leaf.

"Find a plate to transfer this your father's corn meal," she said with a mouthful of bitter leaf. "Good girl," she commended her, "your hand washes bitter leaf well. Anytime I'll cook bitter leaf soup, I'll send it down to you to wahs."

She has given her aunt and forgotten her grandfather. "Is it because domesticated house animals are never as prized as their wild counterparts?" He asked.

Ginika didn't fail to understand her grandfather's request for some bitter leaf which she promptly brought.

Nnenna took a cup of water after eating her bitter leaf. She was still pouring dozens of praises on Ginika as she prepared to go down to her traders and carriers at the market.

"Father, I don't know what is wrong with my memory."

"What is it this time?" Mazi Okwundu querried.

"I nearly forgot the most important part of my mission to this place," answered Nnenna as she brought down her small basket of food and plates. "Father, what does a dream about the royal python stand for?" she asked.

"It means that the owner of the royal python is sending a message to you. How did you see it?" he sought more information.

"It just blocked my path as I was going to get firewood. That was all. I tried to make it go away but it persisted so I had to go back and take another route to the firewood bush. Then I woke."

"Maybe there was danger in the bush waiting for you and Idemili, the god who owns the royal python didn't want you to go there. I'll consult the oracle so as to know the exact form of the message. But it may require some money," Mazi Okwundu didn't forget to include.

Nnenna knew her father too well and was already bringing out some money for Kola, alligator pepper and chicken when her father added the last bit of information. She knew her father had a lot of chicken to spare but he never did anything without a price.

"Go to your market and fear neither man nor demon. I'll see the priest. Nothing bad will ever happen to a good daughter of Idemili, the good daughter that brings her father food," Okwundu reassured his worried daughter.

"You"ll send me a message over the outcome, won't you?"

"Just don't worry. If a sacrifice is required, I'll do all and tell you how I did it. Everyghing will be alright, don't worry."

Nnenna thanked her father who wished her luck in the market. She then left for the market. She took the short-cut foot path that led to the main road. She had just embraced a close relative when she heard the children singing:

> "Nwukpo, Nwukpo, nee kwo ndi uka o,
> "Nwukpo, Nwukpo, nee kwo ndi uka o,
> Onye ya aga kwonu ka o gaba kwo,
> Nee kwo ndi Uka o.

they sang in an array of voices.

Nnenna instantly knew they had sighted a royal python.

The royal python was the totem of the Inwelle people and some villages around. It belonged to the Idemili god to whom Inwelle people also belong and worshipped. The royal python was revered by the people who treated it with all respect. It was never harmed or even insulted though it could be rebuked if it became stubborn and mischievous. It was never killed and if killed accidentally, the culprit made sacrifices at the Idemili shrine. Failure to appease its god, like eating it, resulted in death. Were it to die naturally, who ever saw it will cover it with leaves and anyone that passes by does likewise. People carried it in bags and even around their waists. It kept some people, mostly old ones, company without complaints. If however, it enters a house with a lot of little children, it was carried out into the bush either with the hand or with a long stick. It never bit anyone deliberately and when it did, its bite was never poisonous. The guilty python was then flogged with a single broom stick and severely reprimanded.

Such reverence was as well accorded the related boar constrictor. But because the boar is more deadly, it was usually fed with a goat. While it rested after the tiresome meal, long, strong sticks were tied parallel to its body and it was then taken away into the largest forest around. It was never killed.

Only the newly converted Christians showed disrespect to the royal python with uncomfirmed consequences. But because the church people show open hostility to it, the royal python was allegedly reputed to avoid them by all means. Hence, when it was seen, children sang, warning it of the arrival of Christians who may not be in sight.

As she approached, she discovered that a well-fed royal python was lying across the foot path. Despite the song of the little children that church people were around, it remained adamant and sunbathed itself.

"What have I done to you, Idemili's python, that you bar my way?" Nnenna asked the python. "I've given my father money to appease you so let me pass before I bring a cane."

Nnenna pretended to search for a cane which wouldn't have been a difficult search. The python seemed to hear her clearly and started moving slowly as if reluctantly.

When it had created enough space, Nnenna made a brief detours into the bush on the other side of the path and ran across the trail of the royal python. The python did not stop but continued on its journey into the bush.

Nnenna continued hers towards the market, greeting and embracing virtually everybody on her path.

* * * * * *

A lot of people heard the shrill voice ringing like ten town criers' gongs as it made its way through the thick equatorial forest vegetation. The owner of the voice was in apparent agony because the cry continued with undiminished ferocity. If anything really changed in the tempo of the cry, it was on the increase. Only one thing could cause such grief to an Inwellian; only death could. Whoever heard that voice prayed that the source should not be known to him and, if known, to be remote. Each prayed that the deceased should be alien to him. When Mazi Okwundu first heard the shrill voice, he prayed as others did. But the cry continued to grow louder as the source approached nearer Okwundu. As it came nearer, a dozen other voices joined it and helped convey its message. Occasionally, Okwundu heard a male voice shout:

"Ebeeo; Ebeeo; Ebeeo;
Ndi be anyi, alu melu," which was a model cry for men.

It soon became evident to Okwundu that most people in their vicinity were known-well to the source of that cry. He changed his prayer to the effect that the source should be remotely known to him. He only realised that both God and Idemili had ignored his prayer when he recognised the voice.

"Isn't that Ogonna's voice that I'm hearing?" he asked nobody in particular. Nobody bothered to answer. He stood up and sat down again, clasped his two hands over his face for concentration and divine inspiration. The only inspiration he received was from the only word Ogonna could utter before she became unconscious.

"Nnenna, Nnenna, Nnenna," she said as the grief took over her and she passed out.

Okwundu, his waist pain gone jumped the dwarf mud wall surrounding the entire compound and fell into a shallow pool of mud water. He jumped out like lightning and defying the heavy downpour, headed for the market with his matchet raised high.

"Okwundu," his immediate senior brother, Udemba, called him. "Are you going to fight against death which has taken our daughter, or our forefathers who have allowed this to happen to us or our gods who didn't bother to warn us? Act like a man, let's go back and prepare for the arrival of her corpse. The devil has done its worse."

Okwundu stood stiff on his track and a thousand thoughts and stars criss-crossed the brain under his grey hair-covered skull. Then he bent his head, stood crest-fallen and fiddled with his matchet.

Udemba walked up to him and held his shoulder.

"We even have a danger in our hands; Ogonna, heavy with baby, has passed out, we need help to revive her."

Okwundu reluctantly turned round and followed his brother back to the compound where they learnt that Ogonna had been revived and had put to bed immediately on revival.

Udemba ordered that both Ogonna and child be rushed to the native doctor that acted as "Midwife".

Okwundu refused to remove his wet dress but sat down on the spot and shook his two legs. Udemba and all his other brothers, cousins and friends came and sat around him.

In several rooms in all the houses in the compound and even outside, scores of women wept their eyes out for the rich, beautiful kind lady.

Some grown-up cousins of Chinelo took her away and kept her busy with an incessant supply of akara balls and moi moi. She never had it so good and inwardly prayed that everyday remain like that day.

With more composed people coming down from the market, the full story of what befell Nnenna became known.

* * * * * * *

Nnenna arrived at the market to discover that market was as good as ever. Her customers came in great numbers and each came with an ever increasing amount of produce. She was delighted as she chatted with a dozen of them, embraced one couple after another before retiring behind her umbrella to have her breakfast. It was during this breakfast that the first indication came that the first rain had reached the ground. The wind seemed to blow from all direction as the trees didn't seem to be bending to a definite direction. The big trees in the market resisted desperate attempts by the wind to undo them. Some of them instead preferred to give a few fruits or/and branches to appease the god of the wind. At her breakfast table, Nnenna enjoyed her meal and as well, the game of fighting for the possession of her rainbow - coloured umbrella with the strong wind. As the wind was about to gain the possession, she gave up her breakfast and fought and won the battle for her umbrella.

"I would have finished this meal long ago," she complained to the wind and to herself, but how could I ignore all these friends and relatives. They are just too many but unfortunately too big and important to ignore without attracting their annoyance, enmity or envy. What should one do but to try one's best." She continued as she washed her hand.

It then occurred to her that if it rained the whole market would be thrown into disorder. She had no alternative than to rush around and do her domestic purchases before it started to rain.

She first went to the area where soup condiments were sold. There, she bought some fermented castor oil seed, and vegetable before she went down to the area where they sold akara balls which she intended for Chinelo and her brothers' sons and daughters.

She had finished paying for the balls and had straightened to go when she heard people shouting. She could hardly lift the umbrella from her head when tragedy struck. She never knew what the shout was all about; she never knew what hit her.

* * * * * *

The youths of Inwelle immediately went into action chopping up the trunk of the palm tree which had given way at the base. Many thatched market sheds were demolished and a lot of people were trapped. When all the trapped people were salvaged, virtually all sustained injuries but only one was dead; the victim was Nnenna who was badly trapped among the fronds of the palm tree with the rainbow colour of her umbrella still radiant. Before she was extricated from the mesh of thorns, the news of her death had already spread to Ogonna, who, not bothering to find out the details, traced her way home with the news and her grief. That was the news she took along as she bathed herself uncontrollably in the flood water as frequently as the grief couldn't allow her to keep standing.

Unknown to her and her initial audience, the youths of Inwelle chopped up the entire tree trunk and extricated Nnenna's badly hit body from the mess. They instantly made an improvised coffin with the palm fronds from the cause of her death and threw her remains into it. Amidst cries from all and sundry, two strong young men carried her on their heads on her last journey to her husband's home.

At the boundary between Inwelle and Guru, a delegation from her husband's pre-informed Guru people took over the burden of carrying her remains to Ogbolu's house.

There she laid briefly in state amidst much wailing from all including Udego, Ogbolu's sister and Ogbolu's second wife.

"It is better she were alive as my enemy than dead," Ogbolu's second wife wept bitterly, "my husband's wife, what have we done to you that you have decided to treat us like this," she moaned.

The wailing was still continuing when those males performing her last rites were through and ordered that the corpse could then be moved away to her father's home for burial as was the custom. Not even the increased wailing could stop the two young carriers from doing their job. The did it well and, despite their body being drenched in a mixture of blood and rain water, carried her corpse to the boundary in a record time of less than an hour.

At the boundary between Inwelle and Guru, the corpse changed hands once more and Nnenna's final journey was on.

"What of her fish basket and her pot?" one of her cousins asked on their way home.

"Nweke is carrying them in front," a voice told him.

"And the goat?" he persisted.

"I saw it handed over but I don't know who is holding that one," the same voice volunteered.

* * * * * *

"What did I do to you my forefathers and my personal god that you should dish me such a foul game," Okwundu lamented when he saw the corpse of Nnenna.

"Have a firm grip on yourself, my man, otherwise, we may not be able to cope with the temptation that has befallen us," Udemba advised fatherly.

That evening, they buried Nnenna in the family's farmlands where their ancestors were buried, the fish basket and water pot were sent to the grooves of Idemili. The goat was used to perform certain rites. Thereafter, the blood and some hair were sacrificed to the oracles while the few who waited patiently ate the more delicious flesh and bone marrow.

For weeks and month sympathizers, friends and well-wishers paid condolence visits to Mazi Okwundu who was frequently surrounded by his other brothers, friends and well-wishers. Each visitor advised him on how to endure the loss, a thing he had been telling others which, he was sure was useless because there was nothing anyone could do to death than to endure grudgingly. But despite the cosy company, palm wine bonanza and redundant advices, the shock of Nnenna's death never left Okwundu. Frequently he would be seen staring at an invisible object in the heavens. And not even Udemba's rebuking advice could stop him.

Meanwhile, Chinelo was sent back to her father quite ignorant of the occurrence. Her innocent enquiries about her mother were usually answered with the reply that she went to an unidentified market. She usually took the answer in good faith. Her father was very fond of her and her stepmother tried so much to be nice. Her grandfather and grandmother adored her.

But her departure from Mazi Okwundu's house increased his melancholy. He became more withdrawn and nonchalant until the naming ceremony for Ogonna's premature baby. The baby was supposed to be named by Udemba as the head of the family. But, because the baby was Okwundu's direct grandson, he consulted Okwundu.

Okwundu thought over the issue for quite a long time.

"Are you still with me?" his worried brother enquired.

"Call him Egwuonwu," was the brief reply.

"I've warned you to take this problem a bit lightly. You have no cause to be afraid of death because you have not done anything that the land forbids."

"So hasn't my daughter."

"Okwundu, Okwundu, Okwundu," Udemba called. "I think I've

called you thrice. Wipe your two hands over your eyes, and remove the hands of a monkey from the soup because it resembles those of a human being. I've warned you. You can then do anything that pleases you. The child should be named Egwuonwu, but I'm afraid that a centipede has stung you into being a woman."

Okwundu didn't answer but watched cooly as his brother stood up to go.

"I'll be sending your wife and my two wives to come and condole you," he abused him.

Okwundu ignored him.

So, the child was named Egwuonwu.

Egwuonwu was an uncommon name which only the new baby was known to bear. It was shortened form of Egwuonwu na-atum (I'm afraid of death). It was a name given at the spur of the moment. It reflected the feeling of that period which wore off with time. Three months later, Okwundu wished he had given the baby another name because people kept on referring to him as "that man who is frightened by death." And at that time, he was no more frightened by death. In fact, he had event forgotten or thought he had forgotten much about the cruel death of his daughter. He would have forgotten early enough has Ogbolu's second wife not added pepper into his bleeding wounds.

* * * * * * *

"What have you been doing ever since I went to the market," Ogbolu's second wife asked the four-year old Chinelo.

"I was playing with my sister behind the house," Chinelo answered with the meekness and gentle innocence that would have evoked pity for a half orphan.

"Go and play on," she ordered the poor girl who ignorantly thanked her before she added, "and that is what you'll eat today."

Her step-sister, about her age, received no such rebukes. Though she was eventually fed, it was either very late, poorly or both. But the hankering was incessant. Her step-mother rebuked her for virtually everything to a point that her grandparents frequently intervened on her behalf. Ogbolu saw most of what was happening but no amount of appeal to her wife could stop her from shouting at the small girl. Soon,

Chinelo became melancholic and jumpy. She seldom did anything right, looking frightened at even the slightest sound. She became sickly and emaciated while her formally radiant skin became tarnished and dirty-looking. Her father looked on as if his hands were tied.

Then came the New Yam Festival. It was usually a period of merry-making. Friends and relatives were invited and whoever attended never went back without a story of what he saw. Lines of nice yam tubers were untied and goats and the accursed chicken were despatched to their forefathers in great numbers.

It was only routine that Mazi Okwundu should invite Chinelo, his granddaughter. This he did but the sight that greeted his eyes were not worthy of discussion. He held the smiling girl to his chest as she innocently recounted one thing which they did or another. Mazi Okwundu couldn't hold back tears coming to his eyes. He gritted his teeth menacingly as he answered her "yes, yes . . .," until the word lost its meaning.

"Papa, is it true that I'll be living here with you?" she once asked.

"Nobody is going to take you away from here anymore. You are going to live with your grandfather," he found himself asserting even though he hadn't consulted Ogbolu, her father.

"Wife," Okwundu beckoned his wife without success. "Woman," he repeated before a sobbing Unaku appeared. She was too aged to take proper care of a little lively kid as Chinelo but she wanted to.

"This is not a question of giving her food thrice or more daily but I want where he'll have other children to live and sleep with so that she'll grow up properly. She's still your granddaughter but of your four sons' wives, choose one before the festival is over who'll take direct charge of her."

"There are not two. Only Ogonna can do it well. The others are always restless. They haven't looked after their children well let alone looking after another's."

"It's enough. I didn't call you here to come and peel your son's wives. Go and call me Ogonna. Don't forget to put enough food for me and her at dinner."

Okwundu shook his two legs and supported his chin in his hands as he thought how best to deal with Ogbolu and his people for maltreating the child.

"Father, they said you are calling me," Ogonna announced politely as she was known to do frequently.

"You have two children now. The first is about six years now and the boy, God keep him is about two. Whatever I might have done to you, try and forgive but treat this girl as your third child. If you know anything you would have done for me or her mother do it for her. Whatever you do for your own children, do it for her. You can go."

Ogonna burst out crying when it dawned on her that Ogbolu's people had been maltreating four-year old Chinelo.

"My son's wife, I've not called you here to remind me of what I have forgotten. Please go with her."

Ogonna cursed the Guru people as she carried the confused girl down to her hut.

"Things will never be good for these wicked Guru people. Chei! abomination, they will die of abomination. Let Idemili not allow them to wake tomorrow morning," she cursed.

People were surprised to hear the voice of the characteristically peaceful Ogonna at such hour of the day.

"What is it, my mother's mother," one of the older wives asked her.

As many as all that heard her story joined in heaping insults and curses on the Guru people who were ignorant of the waste of energy and saliva of their Inwelle in-laws.

Arinze, Ogonna's husband came back late in the night as Okwundu ate with Chinelo whom he sent for during dinner.

"I've finally decided to keep this baby back here after the festival," he informed him.

Arinze had only to look at Chinelo once to find out why.

"That is a sound decision. Hand her over to my wife to look after her," Arinze offered.

"I've already done that. No other woman shall do it better."

The father and his son discussed plans for the new yam festival but most of the time Arinze's eyes were rivetted on Chinelo. His father's thought was as well there. Both thought of how much she had changed.

After the New Yam Festival Mazi Okwundu sent message to Ogbolu to the effect that he wanted to keep Chinelo for sometime before she eventually returns home.

Ogbolu sensed the plan and the reasons behind it. He didn't want to be considered a bad father so he flatly refused and said that instead Chinelo might return to her grandfather's home after she must have come back from her initial journey for the New Yam Festival.

"So, he had the courage to say as much?" Okwundu asked the messenger.

"He was spitting fire and raining curses."

"That is the worst he could do. If he dares send anybody here again, I'll deal with him and his messenger so that he sees with his two eyes," Okwundu threatened.

Good sense prevailed and Ogbolu neither came nor sent anybody. He was even glad that a source of discontent had been voluntarily removed from him.

After six months sojourn at Inwelle, Chinelo's beauty re-appeared. She turned out to take all the beautiful features of her mother; her face, voice, height, polite manners and her father's light complexion. She was exceptionally beautiful, then fair in complexion; she was more beautiful than her beautiful mother. Everybody admired her but it took time for the fear created by her step-mother to leave her. Fortunately but regrettably, she seldom mentioned her mother and it was doubtful if she ever remembered her or what she looked like.

On several occasions, Okwundu saw Nnenna in those calm gentle face of her beautiful and peaceful granddaughter. He equally heard her in her voice. It gave him great joy though it frequently invoked very sad memories of the death of her mother.

Chinelo's presence also changed Mazi Okwundu's behaviours towards her sons' wives as a whole and his own wife. He used to be very stingy to the effect that he never spared anybody a single tuber of yam no matter how diseased the tuber might be. He frequently roasted some for his consumption and sold off many for money. No amount of complaint could change him. But with Chinelo around Ogonna received an ample supply of yams, and even money, each Afor market day when he usually sold his yams.

Chinelo never had any problem and soon grew into a beauty. She was so integrated with life at Inwelle that people and even she never remembered that she was from Guru. But the trained eyes of some elders didn't forget.

"Are you not our daughter's child," a man once asked her.

"Yes, I am," she meekly answered.

"I would have said. I'll never mistake that face even if I saw it in a dream. Do you know me?" the intruder asked.

"I'm not so sure," she replied.

"You won't know me, my child. You were too small then when I knew your mother," he added as if knowing her mother had anything with her knowing him. "Greet me, anywhere you see me for I am your uncle," he pleaded.

Chinelo felt embarrassed after that interview but it became quite routine so she got used to it and grew up with it.

* * * * * *

Mazi Okwundu and his son Arinze had sat down to polish off the remains of gourd of palm wine Arinze bought in the morning. They were returning from a family meeting called by one of their relatives who alleged that another relative had cultivated his yams beyond the common boundary. The infringement involved was less than a foot wide. They had agreed that the accused really exceeded limits but that his error was not beyond tolerance. They considered it a common error and asked the accused to own up his error which he did. It was an abomination to up-root planted food crops so he was allowed to keep the strip he stole from his brother. But to appease the complainant, his wife was advised to plant cassava stem along the strip so that when the accused had harvested his yam, the strip will revert to the complainant.

After the arbitration, all were happy as they devoured the large keg of palm wine which the complainant used to present his case. The atmosphere was very cordial belying the fact that the gathering contained some belligerents. It also meant that the case was judged to everybody's satisfaction. When each had taken two cups of the strong stuff, some brought down their basket of stories and gossips.

"Have you people heard the one I heard this evening," one of them asked as he began to unwrap his first packet of gist.

"What is it?" an array of voices asked simultaneously.

"Do you remember that Obiaja man that was fined by the red cap chiefs because it rained the day he was initiated?" he further asked.

"The one that was initiated about six months ago?" one asked for clarification.

"What happened?" yet another asked begging for the obvious answer.

Their informant laughed rudely for quite some time. "He died just this afternoon," he added coolly, "and his son and relatives are running around borrowing money to perform the funeral ceremonies so a as to save the family name."

"What happened to him," a relative, who had been drinking when he released the news, foolishly asked.

"I said he died this afternoon," the informant repeated.

"How did he die because we never heard he was sick," one asked.

"He just came back from farm, sat down on his earthen seat, fell back and was no more."

"Maybe, he was beaten by spirits in the farm," Okwundu suggested.

"That could be true as was the case of the Ozalla man that sold his son to be initiated," Mazi Ngwu added. "That is why this Ozo title never appeal to me because people commit all sorts of crimes to get money to initiate. Only God knows what he did to get the money with which he got himself initiated, a poor palm wine tapper not better off than my humble self."

"No one dies naturally nowadays," Udemba, the only red cap chief among them defended his group. "You people are just jealous. Poverty and stinginess are just your basic problems. After all, what does it cost to get initiated." He went further to enumerate all the other non-red cap chief Inwellians who died under similar circumstances. "Those who have no money for pork always complain that pork causes running stomach. It doesn't cause them running stomach when someone buys it for them. If you people are through with your meeting and wine, let's dismiss."

Most people, including Okwundu and Arinze were already at the doorway because Udemba's comments had a sour taste; it was never complimentary.

So, both son and father were not surprised when they heard the large sound of ground canon.

"Boom, boom, boom," it sounded from the direction of Obiaja.

"So, it is true that Mazi Okolo is gone leaving that small boy to suffer at the hands of those red cap chiefs who have no sense of pity. They consider nothing but their entitlement. This would still puzzle me," Okwundu complained.

He was still speaking when Unaku ran in to inquire of the cause of the canon shots.

"Ogbuefi Okaa-Omee is dead," he informed her very flatly.

"Who will bury him?" she asked as if her husband had anything to do with the Ogbuefi's death.

"Ask me?" he answered and Unaku took the cue and walked away to inform Ogonna that they had another funeral to attend.

* * * * * * *

Nnaife, Okolo's only grown up son was in a state of hysteria when he heard of his father's death. He was learning the art of trading under an influencial Guru-based trader who never spent a penny without sufficient reason. He informed his master who expressed his pity and gave him a pound for transportation and other minor expenses. That was the only money in Nnabuike's pocket when he arrived at Obiaja.

There were no cries in his father's house or from anywhere for that matter. He couldn't believe that the house where someone had just died could be as peaceful and as silent as a grave. He inwardly prayed that the information he received would have been mis-directed but meant for another person. But on entering the main family house, he saw some relatives sitting silently, saying nothing and doing nothing. It then dawn on him that something very serious had happened.

"My father," he moaned.

A dozen of harsh voices shouted him down.

"Don't you know that he is an Ichie and therefore, his death should not be announced carelessly. Be careful and decide on what we shall do," the spokesman for the family duly informed him.

Nnaife shook violently. They were waiting for directives from him and he didn't know a damned thing about the burial of Ichies. Worse still, even if he had known, he hadn't enough money in his pocket. Nobody ever discussed financial affairs with a dry mouth. He felt lost and confused. He went from room to room, sitting down and standing up. Restlessness took over and he prayed for a saviour.

"Papa, why did you die at a time when I haven't got money?" he kept on asking but his father ignored his silly questions.

"My people," the spokesman announced "I've always known it will end up like this. The entire episode is now turning a shameful act that could tarnish the image of the entire family; let us call our son and ask him of his plans as we are sure that Ogbuefi Okaa - Omee left no money before his death."

"You spoke well," they echoed.

A messenger was sent to fetch Nnaife who was still complaining that his father should have waited until he was freed and have started an independent business.

"Our son," the spokesman cautiously started, "Your father is still at the native doctors but suppose he dies, do we announce it immediately or do we postpone it until you are grown up enough to perform all the rites," he demanded.

"I wouldn't refuse," the confused boy tactfully answered.

"What does that mean, that we announce it now or later?"

"Did I refuse?" he stubbornly answered.

"So, let us announce it now," the spokesman offered.

"Did I refuse?" he maintained.

"So we shall announce it this evening," the spokesman pressurised him.

"I wouldn't refuse," Nnaife replied.

"Do we contribute money or did he leave you enough money to go about his funeral," the spokesman asked.

"I will not refuse any help," Nnaife sheepishly answered.

"Go away," one elder thundered at him, "and let us discuss important issues." 'Did I refuse? I wouldn't refuse.' Was that all you learnt at Guru? My brothers, I have heard this boy cry and I think he has problems. Our people say that when a man cries, he says 'Ebeeo, Ebeeo, Ebeeo, thrice.' If he exceeds that number, his people should come to his aid because he wouldn't be mourning only his loss but also his poverty. So, let us decide on what to do."

"Thank you, father," the spokesman continued, "that was exactly what I said before that this episode is going to besmear our family's name if we are not careful. I suggest that the funeral be performed without delay so that it will be less costly. The more the delay, the more the number of people who'll hear and come. Besides, things are getting costlier with each passing day. That is my own suggestion."

"That was well spoken," another elder concurred as well as others. "In addition to what you said, it is very apparent to even goats and chickens that both Mazi Okolo and his son have no money for the funeral. So, to save the family's name, we shall contribute money for the funeral but it should be stressed that we are lending this money to be repaid by Nnaife later. This will curb the tendency of poor people like me hanging their bags at points outside their easy reach. I have nothing more to sys."

"He just summarised our feelings," one member said. So, the family agreed to contribute money if only to save their name but that the amount was refundable.

"That was what we decided," the spokesman informed Nnaife after briefing him on their decision.

"I wouldn't refuse", was all he could say.

"So that is how to thank us?" one enquired.

Nnaife breathed a big sigh of relief, looked at the last speaker very steely, "Thank you," he then said before walking out to nowhere in particular.

He hadn't expected the family to be kind in their response to the situation because they had all opposed his father's initiation into the Ozo Society. But he, his son, had insulted then alleging that they were jealous. He knew they wouldn't have spoken of a repayment if he hadn't supported his father's initiation. But then, he was a young boy being blinded by the honour of being called the son of Ogbuefi.

Despite the hasty funeral arrangements, the compound of Ogbuefi Okaa - Omee was packed full by afternoon and many people did not find where to sit or stand. Some had to throng to the village square where each masquerade retired after a visit to the Okolo compound.

There was much dancing and masquerades came from both far and near. Each visiting troupe received the customary chicken as a token of appreciation. Many had some hope that the smoke that was soon bellowing from behind Mazi Okolo's house meant that they'll go with greasy mouths. However, some of the smoke were due to gun shots and canons. Even the ones due to cooking were from meals being prepared for the Ichies and few special guests.

The Ichies themselves, seemed to be aware of the fact that their food was on fire because, they sang and danced merrily to the amusement and entertainment of spectators. It was fun seeing old men who frequently complain of one ailment or another singing and dancing like kids. Their lead singer was a grey-haired man who could hardly see beyond his nose but his voice still rattled like that of the night masquerade.

"Egwu ndi ogalanya . . . Nzo,
Egwu ndi nwelu ego . . . Nzo,
Egwu anyi ji eme nganga Nzo,
Egwu anyi ji ata nta nta, Nzo . . ." he sang to the amusement of the crowd. Other members, strong enough blew their elephant tusks periodically. They even used it to praise each other and to communicate messages.

They had every reason to be happy because they already had a goat to slaughter at hand. That was given them in the morning when they transferred Mazi Okolo's Ozo title to his son who from then became Ogbuefi Nnanyelugo even though he didn't kill any cow but a goat. In addition, the Ichies were entitled to a second goat and chicken after their royal dance. Kegs of palm wine, bottles of hot drinks and basins of food were fringe benefits that were just non-negotiable. Their entitlements were usually beyond their consumption so many turn up with plates concealed in their bags which had become a part of the regalia of red cap chiefs.

When the red cap chiefs had exhausted their scarce energy, they retired to a remote house quite removed from the funeral ground. There, all their entitlements were set out ready for them.

They called themselves title names.

"Ogbuefi Omee - Oka chie," one called the other.

"My father's tiger. It is not easy to be an ichie. If people say it is easy, let them join," the other responded.

"We have shaken the village once again so that people should know that good things are good for this our village," the first ichie noted.

"Let us go in and see what this son of Ogbuefi has in store for us. A worker is entitled to his pay no matter the condition of things."

As they entered the house, they discovered that the groups sharer, the newest member to be initiated who could as well be the oldest age-wise, was assessing the quantity of things given to them. They easily approved the two goats and chicken. Then they approved both the quantity and quality of palm wine and hot drinks. They as well approved the quantity of the different types of food provided but weren't too sure of the quality. The sharer tasted each of the three types of soup and sanctioned them as true to specifications.

"You are approving them as if you entered into each of them to find out the amount of pieces of¡meat each contained. There shouldn't be any sentimentality. Do things as they were usually done." A powerful member suggested.

The old man sharer went out and came back with a dry piece of the back of a palm frond. He dipped it into each of the soup pots trying to feel the bottom, in each case, he failed because the numerous pieces of meat and dry fish blocked the smooth passage of the stick. It meant that each pot of soup was wee-laced with pieces of meat and fish.

"They have passed this simple examination," one announced.

"They are son's of an Ogbuefi so I had expected them to pass," the other concurred.

The sharer then set about the uneasy task of sharing the food. Each member fed sumptuously to his satisfaction. Each ate what he wanted and what quantity he desired. No one complained. They equally devoured their hot drinks and palm wine. But after eating, the food and drinks looked as if none had been touched.

* * * * * *

"What type of funeral is this?" an Inwelle woman asked to nobody in particular, "that people hadn't even cold water to drink. What type of Ichie is this? My brother will never get initiated under this condition," the hunger - stricken woman complained as she raced down towards Inwelle before the worms in her intestine ate through her intestine.

Mazi Ngwu, walking in the same direction as the woman, heard her quite alright but his degree of hunger couldn't allow him to speak. The thought of the distance he had to trek to get home didn't enliven his depressed spirits. If he were a kid, he would have wept for hunger but he wasn't still a kid. Nevertheless, he wept internally as a man but only prayed that the worms in his stomach that had suddenly kept quiet had not found their ways to his heart. He hoped that their silence was real and with good intentions. He hastened his pace to make home quickly. Then he struck his right leg against a protruding tree stump, "Chei!" he exclaimed, "This is good luck but I wonder what type of good luck it should be when worms are after my life." He hastened more slowly. He had passed the old oil bean tree and was counting his steps towards the young breadfruit tree when he heard someone calling him. He loathed any disturbance but if the person was travelling his way, it would make his journey easier.

"Oh, is it you, Ogbuefi Omemgboji?" he asked when he saw who it was.

"Why didn't your brother, Ogbuefi Udemba, turn up?" Omemgboji asked without bothering to answer his questions.

"He has been sick for sometime now but I thought he would have made it," Mazi Ngwu candidly answered.

"Come so that we shall give you something for him," Omemgboji commanded and Mazi Ngwu reluctantly agreed and followed him.

"Ichies and Ogbuefis, I salute you all," Mazi Ngwu said immediately on entering the house, waving his hat in the air. "My hat is no more on my head," he informed them as he put it back, then remembered they easily find faults in people, removed it and stuffed it into his right pocket.

"Was that why you entered our eating place with your left leg?" one instantly asked him as he was about to sit down. "Maybe you are annoyed that we are initiated and you are not so you want to pollute this place with your left leg."

Mazi Ngwu didn't even know with which feet he entered the house. He even wasn't aware of the significance of the two legs. But he had little space for maneuvers and had no alternative than to apologize as abundantly as he could before they imposed a fine on him.

"My elders and owners, I think the sun has really affected my head so I didn't even remember that the Ichies were here. I'm, therefore, very sorry and will remember to be more careful next time."

"Good man," one elated Ichie called him, "rise for we understand the problems of non-Ichies. They have so much to think about the least of which is not hunger." Turning to the sharer, "Give him food so that he'll know where he is."

The other Ichies burst out laughing. Mazi Ngwu managed a short sheepish grin that never came near his heart. He would have declined the food offer but such an action would have tantamounted to being annoyed with the red cap chiefs which in itself, was a serious offence. Besides, his stomach was on fire and no amount of explanation would have appeased the rebellious worms in his stomach. He meekly accepted the plate of food and looked around for where to sit. He wanted to sit with one Ichie who politely asked him to go outside where the other women were. Mazi Ngwu felt hurt but obeyed. He wanted to leave the scene as fast as possible. He hurriedly swallowed his food and returned the plate. He thanked them for the privilege and the honour done him. He waited patiently for their message for Ogbuefi Udemba.

The group that was responsible for the sharing of the two goats and chicken were already busy but it would take sometime. To keep Mazi Ngwu busy, one of the Ichies offered him some wine which the thirsty man readily accepted.

"Have a second cup because a second of everything is usually good for a man," the Ichies suddenly exclaimed.

It was while he was taking this second cup that his lips made a rasping sound with the cup.

"There is nothing I can't see in this town," one of the ichies suddenly lamented. "Imagine a woman sighing after eating our food and taking our wine. This is absurd."

Mazi Ngwu didn't even know he was the person being referred to. He emptied the cup and was busy licking his wet lips when he was openly addressed.

"I mean you, Mazi Ngwu. Why did you sigh? Is that to show the world that we have offended you by honouring you with our food and palm wine? You want us to give you our wives before you'll be satisfied. Let whoever is keeping this man here settle him before he commits an abomination."

Mazi Ngwu was visibly infuriated. Tears instantly came to his eyes as he looked at his persecutor coolly for a period before he realised he was with the red cap chiefs.

"I did not sigh, my chiefs," was all that he could say as he turned to go outside.

"And he is walking out on us," a voice accused.

"I am not walking out on you but I want to stay outside for some fresh air."

They were very glad that at last they had succeeded in infuriating Mazi Ngwu. That was the only way to bring in non little holders into their fold. Where he sat waiting for the Ichies' message, he felt like vomitting their food and wine but they have had him in his testicles and there was no escape. Everything was an offence to the red cap chiefs. There was no solution. There was no way of escape. If they caught one, they've caught one. The only solution was for one to avoid them like leprosy. But they always caught one at their leisure. There seemed to be only one way of avoidance; to join them. If one got initiated, one would be free of all those intimidations for life, and one's children too.

Mazi Ngwu counted the Ichies one by one in his mind's eye. He assessed each one's social and economic status. Only five could be considered to be better off than him. The remaining two dozens or so were either his equals or a shade lower than him by his own appraisal. He tried hard to forget the humiliation but couldn't. The humiliation was just too much and he was determined to avenge. There were several ways of avenging. He could kill all those that humiliated him. But he reasoned correctly that it wasn't easy to take life. It was never in their lineage to murder others. A more plausible way was to join the red cap chiefs by being initiated. He, there and then, swore to get initiated into the Ozo Society by all means.

He brooded over his humiliation until he got home. He acted restlessly and finally took a seat in the dark corner of his house and literally forgot himself there.

His thought strayed to every nook and corner of the world. He sought reason for the treatment he received but found none. He searched his conscience to know if he had offended anyone to merit such a punishment but his conscience was clear. So, his only crime was that he was poor.

"This village is the only one in the world where it is a crime for someone to be poor," he lamented as if he had visited other villages to sample their behaviours. "But I'm not the poorest and I'm going to prove it," he boasted.

He wanted to get initiated sooner than later. He knew it would be easy if he had money. But he equally knew it wouldn't be easy for him to find the required amount. He schemed his best way of approach. He would have sold off all his yams but they weren't much. The previous years harvest was one of the worst he had over witnessed. That was primarily due to bad weather. Very hungry beetles put a final seal on the bad fate of the poor harvest; he had no yams to sell.

"What of land?" he thought.

That was a useless thought he immediately concluded because he hadn't any sizeable personal land. He would have dabbled into the family land but his cousin and uncles were just too powerful for him. Both Mazi Okwundu and Ogbuefi Udemba could withstand a rainstorm when it comes to family problem. He knew his strength and limitations and was clearly aware of the boundary of the two. He threw out the idea as fast as it entered his head.

"Kai!" he exclaimed aloud, "the sort of insult people receive in this world," he said aloud.

"What is it?" his surprised wife asked.

"My wife, an animal without a jaw bone has really dealt with me today." Mazi Ngwu then went further to tell his wife the entire story carefully avoiding those ones that portrayed him as being very greedy.

His wife was mad over the incidence.

"And that is why you are killing yourself with thought?" she asked. "Don't mind those stupid old men. Whenever they see food and wine they start behaving like school children of yesterday. They start saying things that are not written in any book whatsoever. Some of them, like the big fool that just died had nothing but sold virtually their land just to enable him wear two dirty strings around his ankles and put on a red cap like a male agama lizard."

"And hunger and thirst nearly killed people at his funeral," a relieved Mazi Ngwu quickly added.

"Some of them cheated, stole, killed or kidnapped others in order to get rich and get initiated. They should never be imitated. Even if they adorn their caps with all the white feathers in this world, they remain what they were. When they die, they are not buried in the sky but down here," she said pointing towards the soil, "Or was the one you went to mourn buried anywhere else?" she asked.

She got no reply and thought that her husband was with her. Unfortunately, he wasn't dancing to the tune of her drumming. The last word he heard there was "Kidnap". He turned the word over and over several times before concluding that it was his trump card. He couldn't kill, had no land to sell, had no yam to sell as well, had nothing to steal, was not clever enough even if he found something to steal, had no one to cheat or swindle. But kidnap, that was easy enough. It wasn't a serious abomination if it were one at all. If handled well, it was easy and no life is lost. Mazi Ngwu took the diea and swallowed it line, hook and sinker.

But who was he to kidnap? He taxed his not too bright brain for the answer that will solve his simple dilemma. He tore his hair with his fingers as he battled the devil for full control of his brain. At first, his will power held the devil at bay as he sieved through the unwritten list of people he knew. None was an easy prey. Either the proposed victim would be too risky to be kidnapped or too related to him for comfort. About thirty minutes of serious thought led him nowhere. He became despondent and nearly fell asleep in his recumbent position when the devil took over his poor brain and channelled it to a different wavelength of reasoning and the first port of call was Chinelo. Mazi Ngwu nearly jumped from his seat in jubilation. Here was a young girl of about thirteen, gentle and meek. She had long been forgotten by her father who would care less if she died or lived. Her mother was no more. Consequently, she'll not be missed much by any of her direct owners. Only Mazi Okwundu, his relatives and the other children who play with her, would miss her. But the plot would suit his purpose as she was ideal for kidnap. Ngwu felt very relaxed over the entire issue as the major problems in his head to avenge his humiliation seemed well taken care of. He relaxed and took the parcel to Mazi Udemba who was very grateful and gave him some pieces of goat meat.

Mazi Ngwu threw the piece of goat meat into the bush on his way home.

"Look at the type of insult someone should be receiving from these stupid red cap chiefs. Because he is a red cap chief, he thinks he should be giving me pieces of meat by hand as if I'm still a two-year old kid. This insult would end only when I wear my own strings and don a red cap," he mused as he staggered home.

That night, he seldom slept as he battled with another problem; what to do with Chinelo when he kidnaps her. He failed in all attempts to solve this puzzle. He discovered his total ignorance in the art of kidnapping. He, however, came to an important decision and that was that he needed external help to execute his plans.

Mazi Ngwu woke his friend, Ogbuefi Ide from sleep five days after the funeral of Mazi Okolo. Both men had been friends for more than fifteen years. And since they started their friendship it has been waxing stronger each day. Ogbuefi Ide was from the Idagbe village where the soil was very fertile and food was produced in ample quantity. Poor weather rarely affected their crop because they lived near the confluence of two large rivers both of which overflow their banks annually. Both men met when they were very young. Mazi Ngwu and his dancing group had travelled to Idagbe to teach Ogbuefi Ide and his group their new dancing style. The guests were paired to the hosts and Mazi Ngwu was paired to Ogbuefi Ide who was still a "woman" by then. Both had struck it together ever since exchanging gifts and visits especially during festivals.

Immediately Ogbuefi Ide heard the voice, he knew that his friend had arrived and with plenty of problems too because a man does not keep awake all the night in order just to say hello to a distant friend. He was only too eager to help his friend.

"Whatever is due should not be regarded as greediness," Ogbuefi Ide said after hearing his friend's dilemma. "My friend must be initiated one way or another. People overgrow things. I think you have overgrown being insulted because of these tiny strings," he continued, touching the two strings around his ankles.

Mazi Ngwu waited patiently as Ogbuefi Ide stooped low and made for the interior of his complex mud house. He soon reappeared with two small bundles. He threw the first one at his friend's direction.

"Count it," he demanded.

Mazi Ngwu unwrapped the parcel and started counting the dirty pound notes that met his eyes. His hands were shaking while he counted but he didn't have long to count because twenty pounds isn't so much to count unless one had shaky hands.

"It is twenty pounds," Mazi Ngwu solemnly announced.

Ogbuefi Ide nodded in approval and tossed the second bundle in the direction of his ecstactic friend. Mazi Ngwu allowed the bundle to rest where it landed.

"Count that one as well," his friend prompted him.

His hands went to work as fast as they got to the bundle. It took him a longer time to count than the previous one because by now, his shaking hands had turned convulsive as he wondered how on earth someone could have such a fantastic sum of money at that time when the entire world was still in darkness. Such amounts definitely would have been difficult to realise from yam sales alone. But he conceded that his friend was a hard worker coupled with the fact that their soil was more fertile. Besides, Ogbuefi Ide was a righteous man.

"It is twenty pounds as well," Mazi Ngwu announced.

"You said you needed forty pounds, isn't it? There is forty pounds and stop grieving. You can always count on me. And about the repayment, don't be in a hurry to repay. Just do it as freely as you can. I'll never fuss after all that amount is only the scum of my wealth.

"Omeife Ukwu," Mazi Ngwu suddenly burst into life and rained praises on Ogbuefi Ide. "I've never believed in another person and will never give you cause to regret lending me this money. Shake me."

Each man raised his right hand and they struck each other with the back of the palm thrice before shaking.

"Ogbuefi Onye Ide na ebulu aku," Mazi Ngwu called Ogbuefi Ide.

Ogbuefi Ide wanted to respond in like fashion only to remember that Mazi Ngwu had no corresponding name.

"What will your title name be?"

"Ogbuefi Otue Omee," Mazi Ngwu promptly answered.

"Chei, Ogbuefi Otue Omee," Ogbuefi Ide called back, "take another three."

They struck the back of their palms thrice once more before

shaking.

"Things will be alright soon. Don't worry and stop grieving over what they told you. Now it will be your own turn to tell others. Without the humiliation, most people will opt out of the Ozo title."

Then Mazi Ngwu suddenly burst out laughing. Tears came out of his eyes as he laughed uncontrollably. Initially, Ogbuefi Ide looked on puzzled-and after repeated enquiry led him nowhere, he joined in the laughter. After a laughter spell of more than five minutes, Mazi Ngwu shook his head violently.

"Such little things could lead man to do what he never dreamt of doing," he finally said.

"Yes," agreed Ogbuefi Ide.

"I would have sold off all my yam but I discovered I hadn't any left."

Ogbuefi Ide laughed. "Yes, the harvest in your area was poor last year."

"I wanted to sell my land but hadn't any. If I dared touch our family land, Ogbuefi Udemba and Mazi Okwundu could pursue me even to death."

Ogbuefi Ide was still amused.

"And I had nothing to sell and no one to dupe. I even thought of committing murder but shrank from the idea because it is not in our blood to take life."

"Whom would you have killed?" Ogbuefi Ide chipped in.

"Nobody in particular," came the reply. "If I tell you what I decided on, you'll be shocked. I never knew this was the type of thing that leads people into committing heinous crimes."

"What was it?" Ogbuefi Ide tempted him.

"Kidnap."

"That was better than murder after all, the victim is never dead."

"Hmmm, why don't you practice it yourself if you know it isn't too bad?" Mazi Ngwu asked in mocked seriousness.

"Do you know if I do?" Ogbuefi Ide asked with raised eye brows and eyes protruding.

"You may but I can't," Mazi Ngwu replied with resignation.

"And that could make the difference between me and you, between rich men and poor men, between the lender and the borrower,"

Ogbuefi Ide added philosophically, "the difference could be said to be the conscience but I call it lack of courage - cowardice. And that is why some people will always remain rich while others remain poor. I never know you were weak."

Mazi Ngwu couldn't discover much from his friend's voice. He didn't know for sure whether his friend was joking or was sincerely urging him to kidnap a fellow individual. Whichever was the case, he must absolve himself from the allegation of being weak even though he didn't share the opinion that the conscience that determines right from wrong had anything to do with strength and weakness except the strength to defend conscience.

"I'm not weak but I didn't know what to do with my victim after I must have caught him," Mazi Ngwu defended himself.

"Catch him first and I'll tell you what to do with him", Ogbuefi Ide added coldly. "By the way, do you have anyone in mind?" he asked.

"Yes," Mazi Ngwu answered very reluctantly not very glad at the end of their discussion.

"Who?"

"One Chinelo, a distant niece from Guru whose mother died some years ago," Mazi Ngwu informed him.

"A girl? And who is the father?" came more questions. "I don't know his name but he doesn't care for her any longer so she is presently putting up with us at home." Mazi Ngwu was surprised at the steadiness of his voice and renewed zeal in him to go ahead with his previous scheme.

"She was put into your plate by the gods and you are shying away. But I can understand your problems and will help you."

The two men discussed the issues involved and their plans. The plan was as fool proof as any could be and Mazi Ngwu was more than relieved when he stood up late in the afternoon to go back home.

* * * * * *

Ogbuefi Udemba cleaned his right ear with the first finger of his right hand and then, the other ear. Satisfied that the short ritual had kept the channels of his ears open, he inclined his head towards an amused Mazi Ngwu.

"My brother," he intoned solemnly, "kindly repeat what you have just told me," he begged.

"I want to initiate into the Ozo Society," Ngwu repeated very casually.

"Are you joking or dead serious?" Okee Omee doubted.

"I've come to inform you bofore I make it public. I just felt it would be a slight on you, the only titled man in our family if I make it public without informing you. Besides, you shall be leading me in."

"If a sheep intends growing horns, let it first make sure that its skull is tough enough. Have you considered the cost and made sure you can carry the burdens of the ceremony? Can you tolerate the headaches of these our titled men?" the Ogbuefi enquired with serious doubts.

"Here is the money," Mazi Ngwu said laughingly as he fiddled in his bag for the two bundles of money.

"No," Ogbuefi Udemba stopped him and blocked his movement with his hands. "I've never doubted your wealth. After all, you are an able son of an Ogbuefi. Aren't you the owner of the large piece of land cleared on the way to the stream for yam? Aren't you the owner of the cultivated parcels of farmland along the community farm? Can anyone count your chickens and your goats? No, I'm not doubting your abilities but I thought things are presently very hard judging from the fact that last year's harvest was a disaster. But I seem to forget that you've been selling yams since I knew you and last year was the only bad year."

"I thought you were doubting me. You know I always believe in doing what people see," Mazi Ngwu boasted.

"Great warrior," Ogbuefi Udemba suddenly called him. "Wait, I'm coming."

Mazi Ngwu waited patiently while Ogbuefi Udemba went into his dark room and soon emerged with an unfull bottle of local gin. He poured an insignificant quantity into his shot and poured it on the floor drop by drop as he thanked their forefathers for answering his prayers.

"I've always prayed that I'll have a second person from this family for support so that our share outside should be much. Besides, when I'm speaking I'll do so with confidence and whatever I say should have weight. Take three from me," he urged Ngwu.

They struck the back of their right hand thrice before they shook.

"Ogbuefi ehmm, ehmm, what should be your title name? You've not told me."

"Ogbuefi Otue Omee," Mazi Ngwu answered exuberantly.

"Ogbuefi Otue Omee," Ogbuefi Udemba called him, "you are a strong man indeed. But I hope you didn't take my attack on you people at the family meeting serious. It was directed at certain people. If you had taken it seriously, kindly forget it. I hope this your plan is not as a result of that my comments."

"No, No, No," Mazi Ngwu objected, "I made my plans long before that meeting. That was why I attacked the wretched ichies but not the Ozo institution. That was why I was annoyed because you categorised me among those who were stingy."

"I've already told you that I had an eye on certain people when I made those comments. I've always known that you'll join us sooner than later. You can always recognise a ripe corn by sight. I'll support your entry to the fullest. It still remains one person who I expect to join us soon. You'll discover that person in no time," Ogbuefi Udemba boasted.

"I know the person but he'll be my junior when he enters. I'll take shares before him," Mazi Ngwu prided himself.

* * * * * *

"Have you told Ogbuefi Udemba about this your plan?" Mazi Okwundu asked dejectedly.

"I'm just from his house," Mazi Ngwu glibbly replied.

"What did he say?" Mazi Okwundu pursued.

Mazi Ngwu took great pains to go through the joys Ogbuefi Udemba showed on hearing the news. He cleverly avoided his infused opposition.

"And he agreed?" Okwundu wanted to be sure.

"Yes."

"I can't understand all these. We have too many important things to do within the family and we haven't got money. If I were you, I'll differ this project for a more appropriate period," Mazi Okwundu counselled.

"But I have already informed the Ichies," Mazi Ugwu lied. "They'll never initiate me if I disappoint them now only to reapply later. Besides they'll make fun with the name of our family."

"Whether they made fun or not is not important but where will the money come from? My harvest was poor last season and I simply have no penny left even for the upkeep of this baby they left in my laps," Okwundu complained.

"I saved enough money and hope to have a surplus even. I'm not asking for aid but just to inform you so that you don't have to buy an ear to hear it from an outside source."

"I've heard but consider this thing I told you very seriously and see whether you can defer it a little till after the harvesting season."

"I don't want to postpone it for a single day. I hope to go on with my plans. I've informed you."

"You have and thank you. I won't be the one to stand by your way to being initiated. If others agree and you are sure you are well prepared, who am I to stop you? Who doesn't like good things within the family? But what I dislike is any project that could lead to shame. If you say you are fully prepared and Ogbuefi Udemba is in full support, then count me in. Have you fixed the date yet?"

"Not exactly, but it should be around the eighth month."

"Try and inform the rain makers early enough so that the Ichies don't fine you seriously if a single drop of rain falls on them," Mazi Okwundu suggested.

He had been forced to change his stance so that Mazi Ngwu should not think that his opposition was due to personal envy.

Soon, the news of his intending initiation spread throughout the village. People wondered aloud how he came about the money.

"Is that the Ngwu I know or another one?" a woman farmer asked in surprise when she heard the news.

"Are there two?" her companion asked in reply.

"The brother of Ogbuefi Udemba and Mazi Okwundu," the unbelieving woman persisted.

"That's the one," her patient companion confirmed.

"The one that lives near the big pear tree whose branch fell last year and nearly demolished part of his house?" the still confounded woman pressed on as if the description wasn't enough yet.

"I see you are having some gossip in your mouth this morning. Let us stop so far and do some useful work."

"What do you want me to say when a man who could hardly feed his family three times a day, rose one morning with a serious headache to declare his intention to initiate into the expensive Ozo institution," the still not convinced woman insisted.

"Barely six months ago, he was weeping like a baby over the poor harvest and now he remembers nothing to do with his hard-earned money but to initiate himself into Ozo."

"They said he owns a lot of goats and chickens but I think he sold some of his parcels of land. Only goats and chickens can't initiate a man nowadays even if they fill this village."

"I'm yet to know what grows money for these people," the other woman still doubted.

"Why are we breaking our heads for some other person's problem?" the second woman suddenly asked as she bent down to do some more useful work. "His sister who is being married at Obiaja was dancing in the market the other day over the news. She would have been the right person to worry. And if she is not, why should we?"

"It's just that I hate seeing some very odd events. How large is his sister's brain? Wasn't she the one that was telling their dancing group that her husband doesn't give her food money? Is it what a sensible woman should do? Did the others tell her how they manage with their own husbands? She received a befitting hiding from her enraged husband. That is the person you are quoting."

"What do you want me to say when I cannot explain this madness, people preferring ropes on the ankles than food in their stomach or those of their relatives."

"That is their headache. It will only increase the number of hungry men who'll leave behind gigantic problems when they are no more."

"We are living in a world so let's watch and see," the second woman ended philosophically as she urged the other woman to go back to work.

* * * * * *

The happy leaders of the Ichies of the land sat round six large kegs of the best palm wine the town's wine tappers could produce. Their oily faces betrayed their signs of joy that another "woman" had decided to enrich and entertain them thereby swelling their numbers. Ogbuefi Udemba was among the Ichies and couldn't hide his feelings of happiness.

"We have heard what you said, our great Ogbuefi," the spokesman of the Ichies addressed Ogbuefi Udemba, "and we very much understand your enthusiasm to have your brother initiated. But we can't discuss this very important issue with empty mouths. We shall do things in their usual order. Let us first quench the thirsts in our throats by pouring out some of the contents of those Kegs. You are asking us to consider your brother without our confirming whether the contents of those kegs would pass through the throat or just the fluid of the plantain stem. We shall taste it first so, call him to come and serve us for it is not easy to be a senior Ichie. If he thinks it is easy, why didn't he enrol earlier? Let's see him."

Ogbuefi Udema beckoned his brother who had been waiting under a tree outside the house.

Mazi Ugwu ran down to the house. As he got to the door, he waited for a split second as he adjusted his steps so that he doesn't enter with his left leg.

"Are you peeping at us or are you suspicious of our activities here?" one of the Ichies didn't fail to accuse him.

"No, my Ichies, I was adjusting my step so that I should enter with the right leg," he answered humbly.

"You wasted too much time so I thought you were having second thoughts. If it is so, you can have back your kegs of wine," another attacked.

"My Ichies," Mazi Ngwu defended, "My hat has fallen off my head." He gestured with his left hand as if he was removing a nonexistent hat off his unprotected head. "The kegs are for you. I can never have second thoughts," he boasted.

"We are prepared for you tough Ichies," Ogbuefi Udemba came to the rescue of his brother. "This is only the beginning. Has anybody ever used six kegs of palm wine to indicate his intention to initiate? My brother is well fortified with money. This is only the beginning. We have not even arrived," he boasted.

Mazi Ngwu, much relieved went on to serve his tormentors.

"Shake it well so that the dregs will mix well with the ordinary wine before you serve me," one commanded.

Mazi Ngwu amused by the troubles and demands of the Ichies did as he was ordered and gave the Ichie a full cup.

"Ehmm! It is now that you can get the actual taste of the wine."

Others greedily swallowed theirs and asked for the shaken variety.

"Kindly give me a third one and then I can hear you properly. Our people say that people don't discuss important issues with two cups of wine in their heads. But with me, three cups do me a lot of good and with this type of wine, even four won't do me much bad."

"You can go outside now so that we can discuss your fate," said one Ichie after taking delivery of his fifth cup. "No, stay and tell us what this wine is all about. We have heard from Ogbuefi Udemba but we did with one ear because a snake killed by a single individual usually turns out to be a royal python. We want to hear from the masquearade himself because the closest relative of a dead man bears the corpse over the head region and leads the way. Speak for we have important things to do today."

Mazi Ngwu diligently went over all that Ogbuefi Udemba had told his colleagues with all humility and reverence.

"And you have assessed yourself and feel you can bear the burden?" one sleepy-eyed Ichie asked as he battled with the sensation seeping through his brain.

"I did my home work very well," Mazi Ngwu answered.

"Alright, let's hear you. We can't kill a tortoise and keep the boiled meat overnight. If you are prepared, act."

Ogbuefi Udemba put his hand into his goat-skin bag and produced the tied bundle of money. He tossed it to the head of the Ichies.

"Give it to him to unwrap," he demanded," I can't act as his servant! Even the chief doesn't have an Ichie as his servant."

Mazi Ngwu bent down and untied the strings around the parcel. He extracted the money and handed them back to Ogbuefi Udemba who then handed it back to the head of the Ichies.

Mighty smiles spilled over the faces of the Ichies as their leader counted the money.

"It's twelve pounds," he announced to the gathering.

"It is correct," they answered him.

"You have acted like a man," he praised Mazi Ngwu, "shake us." Mazi Ngwu shook each of the Ichies and thanked them for honouring his appeal.

"There is no more problem. You have performed your own part very well. We shall show you a sample of how we act in the society," he was assured. "But it has not finished," he was duly reminded. "You'll meet us here in two native weeks time so that we fix a date for your Iju-alor. If you ever change your mind, let us know though we are sure you won't. You should also remember that after the Iju-alor nothing, not even your death would stop us from initiating you. So, think well and let us know what you feel before then."

"What I feel today is what I'll feel then," Mazi Ngwu boasted. "There is no going back."

"Ogbuefi ehum, ehum, . . ., what should be your title name?" one asked.

"Ogbuefi Otue Omee," Ogbuefi Udemba.

"Otue Omee O O," three of them called him simultaneously.

"Let it be as we have planned," one added.

"I think we have finished for today?" another asked.

"Yes, except that he should take two kegs for himself and Ogbuefi Udemba. We shall be returning your kegs to you in the morning."

Mazi Ngwu wanted to object because the kegs didn't belong to him. Besides, the owner should be needing them for his evening collections. But he dared not oppose the Ichies. Instead, he told them that it was no problem but went down home still battling on what he'll tell the owner of the kegs.

The Iju-alor part of the Ozo in initiation was the most important and most probably, the most expensive. Everyone looked forward with repressed doubts to find out how poor Mazi Ngwu could cope with such a costly project.

* * * * * *

Mazi Ngwu sat on an up-raised seat in front of his house. On two of his sides but slightly behind him were his brothers Mazi Okwundu and Ogbuefi Udemba. Among them were friendly Ogbuefis and well-wishers who had come to lend support to Ogbuefi-to-be Ngwu's initiation.

By Mazi Ngwu's side, was a small wooden mortar full of shilling coins. Mazi Ngwu smiled radiantly at the crowd that had come to honour him. He felt so relaxed and confident in his white agbada dress. But the raging tension within him could be assessed by the unrestricted amount of sweat that soaked his armpit, seat, palm and forehead. He fought it courageously with his large cow-hide hand fan which was aided occasionally by a dirty rag that stood for a handkerchief.

The arrival of any new Ichie was heralded by a noisy exchange of cat-calls as both sides, the hosts and the guests, tried to outdo the other in praises and greetings.

"The son of wealthy man," Ogbuefi Omee Okachie called out as he arrived.

"Ogbuefi Omee Okachie," Mazi Ngwu responded. "The dwarf bull that sends a pack of giant ones on the run."

"The son of an Ogbuefi," Omee Okachie continued.

"The powerful gun powder that destroys the gun," Ngwu countered.

"The bad dog that warms its body over the fire with his head."

"You are that bad bone that people speak of. Whoever eats you without care only gets choked."

"We have arrived," Omee Okachie announced, "to know what you great men have in store for us."

"We've been waiting for you people. We told you that we are well prepared but it seems as if you people doubted hence you came late. But we waited for you knowing that whoever waits for his guests in his house seldom suffers from waist pain. Sit down, let me give you a piece of fish for you know I'm from the land of plenty."

Ogbuefi Omee Okachie busied himself with exchanging a similarly noisy greeting with Ogbuefi Okaa Omee as they hit their large cow-hide hand fan thrice with their backs and once with their fronts.

When Ogbuefi Omee Okachie straightened up, Mazi Ngwu handed him his own Iju-alor share of two shilling and six pence.

"Ogbuefi Otue Omee, the dwarf palm tree that fills keg with palm wine," he praised Mazi Ngwu." My father once told me that whenever a great masquerade visits a great house, in a great town on a great occasion on a great market day, surely a great present will be its reward. I now believe. From now on, you have no more problems," he solemnly announced with the authority of a king.

"I told you we were prepared," Ogbuefi Okaa Omee chipped in.

"You needn't tell me because I've always been aware of the abilities of this great family. It is only that some of your sons are tainting the good name of your family," Omee Okachie added mischievously as he danced round, found a seat and sat down.

Mazi Okwundu fidgeted uncomfortably on his seat while Mazi Ngwu enjoyed the joke.

Other Ichies arrived in due course and each received his own Iju-alor share. A large amount of money was involved but Ngwu had his solace on the fact that he would recoup his money when other people get initiated though slowly.

When virtually all the Ichies had arrived, they went into a close session where, over kegs of palm wine, they agreed that Mazi Ngwu had fulfilled all his major obligations and was therefore fit to be initiated.

"You know the gravity of what we are going to do now," their spokesman asked Mazi Ngwu when he arrived in response to their call.

"We now assume that you know what you are doing," he continued. "Today is the Iju-alor and the next step is the actual initiation. We'll like you to formally inform us on the date you bear in mind."

"The second Oye market day of the eighth month," he promptly announced.

"That should be three days after the funeral of the chief of Irua people?" one Ichie asked.

"Yes," another answered, "five days before the Umuafor festival."

"We shall kill ourselves with festivals this season," an Ichie rejoiced.

"It isn't our fault that we are Ichies," the spokesman said, "the date is very good. But have you checked to make sure that nothing falls within that period? I'm stressing this because you are aware that nothing, not even your death, that of your child, wife, brother or mother, can change this date. So, check properly."

Mazi Ngwu raised his head up and brought it down defiantly, "Nothing will disturb it," he announced having consulted that split second with his personal god which told him that he or any of his relatives won't die before or during that period.

The Ichies had their drinks and dispersed in wait for the D-day.

The news of the announcement of the date for the initiation ceremony spread as usual like wild fire. And with the announcement, all preparations for the eventual initiation went into top gear. All the houses in the vicinity were thoroughly scrubbed with red earth and fine art patterns made on their walls with white chalk and black charcoal. The playground in front of the compound was weeded and bamboo seats erected at its sides. Within Ngwu's family compound, the renovations were more marked. Old thatched roofs were removed and replaced with new ones. Relatives bought new dresses and the female folk in addition bought armlets and earrings. The young boys had their hairs shaved to the skull while the fairly grown-up girls and the married women spent enormous periods plaiting their hairs into complicated hair-dos. The females in addition made tatoo decorations on their bodies with the African blackwood dye.

Chinelo was not left out in the preparations. Mazi Ngwu sewed her a new dress for the occasion in addition to the one Okwundu produced. Her hair was plaited for her by one of her cousins and Ogonna had her body tatooed for her. She wasn't interested so much with the initiation itself as with the "Egwu Onwa", the night play by Ngwu's friends and relatives. It was usually a night to remember in the life of every young girl. The young girls in particular had really started practising their songs and dances for the "Egwu Onwa". Chinelo was the centre of attraction in these meeting where her voice, which she inherited from her mother, was the envy of all and sundry. She told and retold the stories she would tell during the occasion till she had perfected every word and sentence in the story. Her favourite was the story of an orphan being maltreated by her step-mother. She equally practised the play songs at her leisure.

The atmosphere was, therefore, festive that Afor market day, three days before the actual initiation process, two days before the "Egwu Onwa". Chinelo was in the wave as she sang one of the new songs they were taught on her way to the market.

As she emerged from the path she had created between two huts, she looked in the direction of Mazi Ngwu's house, maybe to get the assurance that everything was still in order. Having been assured by the decorations on Mazi Ngwu's house, she was about to turn on her way when she saw the head for which the cap was being made. He seems to be busy sunning his dresses and dusting his box. But funny enough, he spent most of the time looking on the way going towards Arinze's house. Chinelo was very amused to see her mother's uncle girraffing like a kid. She enjoyed herself for sometime before greeting him.

"Ogbuefi Otue Omee ooo," she called out from behind.

Mazi Ngwu nearly fell off the large stone from which he was looking over the fence.

"Good child," he commended her. "I was looking for someone who'll help me buy Kola in the market. As you have come around, you could as well help me do it," he pleaded. "My wife, sister and children have all gone down to the market to dance round and inform people of the initiation."

Chinelo did not need all these explanations because she considered herself his granddaughter and therefore, should do anything for him as his daughter would. Besides, she was aware of the dancing going on at the market and was really going down there to witness the ceremony. She was moved by her mother's uncles' humility in taking pains to explain to her.

"Run down quickly for I'm expecting visitors. Don't discuss or play on the way. I'll give you a price if you come back before this spit dries out," he baited her as he spat on the floor.

She flew out like a bullet and raced down the market. She was on her way back in no time and was still racing when she was interrupted by a stranger who was asking for the way to Irua village whose chief was dead and his burial had been kept secret until certain rites had been performed because he was an Ichie. Chinelo hastily informed him before running on.

"Good girl," Mazi Ngwu praised a breathless Chinelo as she approached. "Take it inside and drop it at the head of my bed," he commanded without raising his head from the box he was ostensibly cleaning.

The glad but exhausted girl obeyed as she hoped such a commendation was a prelude to her price for returning with despatch. She kept on wondering how much or what her grandfather's brother would give her in appreciation when she got to his bedroom. By then, Mazi Ngwu had looked left and right, but satisfying himself that most of the people were down the market, decided that it was time for action. He whistled loudly to signal the beginning of the actual action.

All of a sudden, two powerful hands appeared from nowhere and gripped her neck thereby choking her. Chinelo never expected such a reception. It wasn't what any young girl would expect from the bed-room of her grandfather. She tried to shout so that her mother's uncle would come to her rescue but the grip was like that of steel. Besides, she was too tired after the race to the market. She opened her mouth for air and got it plenty; immediately she opened her mouth, a stick was placed across her open mouth. A rope was run from one end of the stick to the other and made to pass behind her head. The gag ready, the two hands around her neck released her with much relief. She panted for quite sometime as she wondered what really was happening. She couldn't learn much. She didn't even see the features of her captors well and didn't know them. They themselves weren't bothered as they tied her hands behind her, bound her feet and blindfolded her. They finally carried her into Mazi Ngwu's "ofe", his inner chamber, where nobody, not even his wife, ever enters without his due permission. There, they laid her down besides his carved images of his ancestors and covered her over with plantain leaves.

At first, Chinelo had expected her grandfather to seek her. But when they carried her into his "Ofe", she started entertaining fears that her grandfather's brother could be party to the plot. As it grew dark and he still didn't look for or ask of her, she became convinced that he was in fact party to the kidnap. She wept and wept until tired, she fell asleep.

* * * * * *

"I have not seen this girl this evening," Mazi Okwundu observed as he washed his hands to pounce on his dinner of pounded cassava foo-foo and melon soup. "I've been searching for her with my eyes but without success."

"I've been doing likewise but I don't think she is within the family at all. Some of her playmates have come to ask for her," Unaku responded. "I'll enquire from Ogonna to know whether she sent her anywhere or whether Chinelo told her of any intentions to visit somewhere or to escort somebody somewhere."

On contact, Ogonna proved as ignorant as the others.

"I thought she was over there at the big house," she said. "Let us send people to Ogbuefi Udemba's house and that of Ngwu to know whether she is there. But I'm afraid she isn't used to staying away from this compound all this late. Maybe, she has learnt another habit which I'll cure her when I lay hands on her," Ogonna boasted.

Further enquiry to Ogbuefi Udemba and Ngwu's houses yielded no positive results. Similar exercises to less related homes were as abortive and the search for Chinelo had begun.

All members of their family gathered in Mazi Okwundu's house. Many were crying as numerous theories and hypotheses were propounded, appraised, discarded or accepted for critical analysis and experimental tests.

"I saw her running to the market and back. When I enquired, she breathlessly answered that somebody had sent her to go and buy kola. She never said whether the nameless fellow was a man or a woman. But, the way she was running, I suspected that there was more to it than just buying kola," one distant relative informed the sad crowd.

Before she could finish, nearly all the entire crowd trooped towards the market. They meticulously turned up dry leaves on the way, looked up every tree, scanned every farmland and searched the upturned tables in the market all in search of a four feet seven girl. It later turned up to be a wasted exercise. The disappointed search party dejectedly eventually made its way home where it met another crowd of newly arrived sympathisers.

"I think you people are looking for Chinelo?" a female voice asked. "I saw her on the way to the market, directing one man the way to Irua."

Before she could finish, the entire crowd, misunderstanding her to mean that Chinelo was escorting the stranger to Irua, made their way towards Irua. The search was as meticulous but on getting to the boundary, three able-bodied men were sent across to enquire from friends whether they saw such a girl. The rest returned home a little more despondent.

"This is the handwork of my enemies and those of our family," Mazi Ngwu complained. "They don't want me to get initiated. They want to embarrass the Ichies and tarnish the good name of our family."

"They are wasting their time," Ogbuefi Udemba responded. "After washing their hands, our enemies would only succeed in soiling them once again."

"If I had known that this is what my enemies would do to our family name, I would have left the Ozo for other people," Mazi Ngwu lamented.

"It is enough, stop mourning her before she's dead," Mazi Okwundu protested. "If you have to do things the way your enemies want you to, then you would have died because you first of all stop eating since it will be against their will if you don't."

"What do you want us to say when virtually everything seems to be working against us?" Mazi Ngwu complained.

"Let's move away from these crying women. We need to plan our actions. Let's go over to my house," Arinze suggested.

All the others saw with him and each slowly and silently found his way to Mazi Arinze's house. They agreed to wait till the people they sent to Irua had returned. There was crying as the men arrived at the original spot of meeting. Mr. Okwundu's house. The women started crying when the men returned without Chinelo. They ultimately found their way to Arinze's house when they were informed that the men had moved there. The men were all ears when the three messengers approached.

Many people spread their two palms sideways in enquiry. The leader of the search party to Irua shook his head persistently.

"Nobody saw her," he finally announced, "and we didn't see any trace of her on the way."

"What will I tell my god if this child is not found," Okwundu wondered aloud. "What if this girl was used to bury the dead Irua chief."

"You see! Ask the same question that I asked immediately they mentioned Irua. I had feared as much," Ngwu accented. And raising his voice, "the people of Irua, what have I done to you to merit such a treatment?" He bent his head towards his upraised shoulders, shook his leg violently and gritted his teeth in perfect harmony.

"My brother, take it lightly," Mazi Okwundu counselled. "We have not confirmed anything yet."

"What do you want to confirm again? When you are shown the elephant, you are still looking for its footprints. The case is as simple; the witch cried yesternight and the baby dies today. Who with his right senses should deny that it wasn't the witch that killed the baby?"

"I'm telling you that the fire burnt a white priest and you are still asking whether it burnt his moustach. The story is straightforward enough," one of the younger errand men added.

"I can't believe until I see with my eyes any conclusive evidence," Mazi Okwundu refused to bulge even though others in the meeting saw with Ngwu and the errand man. "I'll go to the oracle. Whatever it says, I'll take. If eventually the people of Irua are responsible." he sighed, "I'll teach them what the fire does with the ear of a rat. I swear by Idemili that I'll not rest until each family in Irua was wearing a black dress as a permanent symbol," he promised.

"We are there," reminded the family spokesman, "you people won't even know when we'll perform the deed when it comes to that. Leave that one to us and they won't live to tell the story of what happened to them."

Ogbuefi Udemba conselled that all should remain calm until the outcome of the proposed consultation with the oracle.

"I think I had better postponed my initiation until we see the end of this. After all one whose house is burning does not go about prusuing rats escaping the fire," Ngwu humbly suggested.

"Impossible," Ogbuefi Udemba exclaimed.

Ngwu sighed as if he had just remembered that not even his death could affect a change.

"I've always told you that you won't live long if you depend on the demeanour of your enemies for your actions," Okwundu rebuked him. "Please do not tell the Ichies that I, Okwundu, advised you to deny them the food and drinks for which they have already sharpened their throat. The problem has got nothing to do with you or your initiation."

* * * * * *

Where she lay, Chinelo woke barely ten minutes after she thought she dozed off. She could hear half a dozen voices mentioning her name at the same time and was convinced that a search for her had already begun. She wasn't too optimistic about the ability of her searchers to locate her. After all, Mazi Ngwu would be one of the last people to be suspected for her abduction. Besides, she was concealed in his "Ofe", a high walled enclosure, a man's chamber of chambers, where no one ever enters without the explicit permission of the owner. The hopelessness of the search then became apparent to her. She felt that the only way she could be salvaged would be by her attracting the searchers. She tried to attract that attention by shouting. She only succeeded in swallowing a choking mouthful of saliva. Her mouth and neck ached so badly that, coupled with the frustration and the feeling of not being wanted, she wept until all the energy left in her body was totally drained. She heard all the talk about her being abducted by the Irua people and wished her people knew half the truth. She still lay there, tired, cold, dirty and hungry the following morning when a delegation was despatched to the Oracle for consultations over her whereabout and fate. She heard people muttering and discussing the fact-finding visit. She felt happy and optimistic that at last her salvation was in sight.

At the front of the same building, another concerned relative, who had been very conversant with the oracle, prayed that the powerful oracle would never be specific but cast a blanket description of the event and the culprit. He knew that, even though the Chief Priest could know the true story, he always avoided the ever present threat of prosecution by avoiding being specific. Consequently, he usually smarted around the facts thereby giving room for multiple and confusing suspicion. He, however, had his heart in his mouth in anticipation of what the oracle would say. It was a possibility, though an uncommon one, that the chief priest could give enough description to make him a serious suspect. To prevent such a disastrous implication, he sharpened his mouth to ward off any suspicion to somebody else. After all, very many people would fit into his description. All he had to do was to shift attention to somebody else before suspicion builds around him. Only one description would shatter his plans; that of an Ichie as being the intended culprit. He shuddered at the thought but had no apparent or immediate solution to that. He only prayed for the best while courageously prepared for the worst. Though nervous, he shored up his morale as he waited for the return of the messenger.

* * * * * *

The chief priest had heard the popular rumour about the mysterious disappearance of Chinelo, the young grandchild of Mazi Okwundu. He was, therefore, not surprised when the inquisitive delegation arrived. But to be on the safe side, he received them formally, broke a piece of kola nut which all of them ate.

"You are free to say what brought you people here when I am expecting you to bring me my own share of the Ozo Cow," he said to the unamused assembly. "I have thanked and appeased our gods and forefathers for today."

The spokesman for the delegation then formally brought down his basket of stories of what happened and their searches so far.

"We have searched in every conceivable corner but with little success. The whole episode is becoming very embarrassing, so the messenger of the most powerful oracle, we need your help."

"You have done well," the chief priest muttered." It's really bad. But I'll do my best so that the culprits do not get away with such a serious crime. Be rest assured that if she is alive, I'll make sure she is returned with minimum delay," he promised.

He took a piece of the broken kola nut, chewed it, went out and spat it all around the root of a large cotton tree which represented the oracle. He then took a mouthful of alligator pepper, chewed it with apparent much discomfort and spat it around the cotton tree root as he did the kola. He poured palm wine as libation to the gods of the land. Finally, he rang a metal bell round the groove inviting the gods to come forward, that the appointed time has come and warning off less powerful gods to hid as darkness has occurred in mid-morning.

When he had satisfied his gods and maybe his whims and caprices,he hurriedly took his seat in front of his shrine, chanted some supposedly mystic terms and incantations. Information started pouring out in torrents which nobody could control or accommodate. The visitors waited and looked on, captivated.

"A titled man, what are you doing with your daughter?" the chief priest asked. "Ichie, the son of Ogbuefi, this thing you are doing is not worthy of the honour people give you fair-complexioned middle-aged father. Go and release Chinelo from bondage because it is an abomination. Hmmm. . .," he chortled. "Chinelo is bound hands and legs. She is in difficulty and pain. She hears all that you people say about her but she cannot speak though her mouth is open. Something must be done hurriedly if she is to be saved."

"Who is holding her?" the leader of the delegation asked.

"Her relative," came the annoyingly brief reply.

"Where is he being held?" the leader persisted.

"In her home," came an equally inconclusive reply.

"And you said that she could hear some of our discussions."

"Yes, she even knows you people were coming here."

"And you said that the relative is a titled man?"

"Yes."

"Middle aged?"

"Yes."

"Her father?" he cornered the chief priest.

"Yes," was the relieved but surprising reply.

"Why did he abduct her?" the visitors persisted.

"For money for the ceremony."

The visitors didn't bother to ask which ceremony but assured they knew. They thanked the chief priest, paid the consultation fees and hurried down home to break the news to their people. The atmosphere was very tense when they arrived. All eyes were focused on their faces and especially, on their mouths, when they entered the compound.

* * * * * *

"I've always known that the people of Guru would do anything for money." Mazi Ngwu pronounced after they have heard from the messengers. He had been shaking violently like the others, when the description of the culprit was being given, but for a different reason. If one had put one's hand into his anus then, one would have touched a lot of oil and the seat on which he sat would have boiled hot water.

He, however, breathed a big sigh of relief when they said the culprit was a titled man and specially, her father. "His father wants to make money by sacrificing her. He thinks she hasn't got anyone to speak for her. We shall give him anything he wants. We shall not stay here arguing while precious time is wasted. We shall instantly send a message to her father to the effect that we want that girl back immediately or one or two things will happen; either they kill us or we kill them. I am ready to renounce the Ozo title to see the end of this thing," he offered.

"That is fine talk but you'll go on with the initiation, now that I know who is having my daughter, I think I can handle this alone. I and the people of Guru are used to each other. Ask them what transpired between us in our last land dispute and they'll tell you that I am not biscuit bone that people eat with ease." He stood up and went into his house. "You can all go to your different homes," he announced from his room.

Mazi Ngwu wiped his brows of a massive mat of cold sweat that had suddenly appeared there. He sighed a second sigh of relief and yawned deeply. He, with others slowly but solemnly, moved away to their homes.

Where she lay, Chinelo wept on hearing the eventual mis-direction of the discussion. Maybe only she, the chief priest, and Mazi Ngwu himself knew the actual culprit. She lamented the weakness of her mother's relatives and their lack of alertness. She could not understand how her people forgot that the oracle had said that she could hear them very well which meant she was near. Besides, she wondered why her grandfathers did not recognise that Mazi Ngwu should be regarded as being an Ichie after he had performed his Iju-alor. She was very much disappointed and weak at the ease with which Mazi Ngwu manipulated his brothers. She prayed that someone would remember the first information and maybe, correlate it with the second.

* * * * * *

The search for Chinelo was intensified in virtually all directions when threats failed to prove Ogbolu or any of his relatives guilty of abduction. Ogbolu's response was conclusive enough.

"My In-law," he said when he met Mazi Okwundu at Inwelle where he had come immediately the two messengers had delivered the threatening message from Mazi Okwundu, "this fartulation done on top of a palm tree by a wine tapper is really confusing to me, the house fly. What really happened?"

"Where is Chinelo?" Mazi Okwundu asked aggressively.

"Where is she?" was the commensurate reply, "she was living with you so you should know better. What happened?"

"We can't find her anywhere," was the sober reply Okwundu involuntarily gave. He then proceeded to give Ogbolu a detailed story of all that happened as far as to what the oracle said.

"I am titled quite alright and am her father. Why should I kidnap her when I can easily come to you and have her back? They said she was abducted for money, what do I need the money for when I presently have money that can never be exhausted? Who doesn't know me in your village that I should come and kidnap a girl of Chinelo's age without notice? Where did I keep her? And the oracle said she is still around which meant that she is in a nearby house. She wouldn't be able to hear a discussion being conducted in Guru from here. Let us be more realistic in our decision and more thorough in our search. She is not far but the oracle would have been more definite. She is not with me and may things never be good for me throughout my life," he collected a handful of sand and before Mazi Okwundu could stop him, emptied a sizeable fraction into his mouth, "and let the soil of your land not allow me get home safely if I have anything to do with her abduction except that of a father in search of his loved daughter."

"I'll prefer to swear by the Iyi-Ojii of Ilabe people or the Udo of the Isoka people. I did not abduct my daughter either for money or for any other reason."

"It is okay. No more swearing in my house. I believe you didn't but under prevailing conditions, one tends to believe everything. More so when the oracle tends to cast doubts over some people. You did not, my in-law. We shall search together."

Chinelo was elated at what she heard but by night, no one came closer to her hiding place than on previous occasions. She wept out of despondency. Her mouth ached so seriously that when her captors relaxed the gag to feed her with water and pap, she prayed that the gag be replaced to reduce the searing pains.

A repeat visit to the oracle the following day yielded not much new information. The oracle gave a verbatim repeat of what it said previously but more importantly, maintained that Chinelo was still within the compound. More confusing was the report that she never knew the hands that apprehended her and that these hands were not those of sons of the land. But insisted that one of her fathers, already described was involved.

"Is this her father from Guru or from Inwelle?" Ogbolu asked impulsively.

"He is not from Guru," the oracle spoke through the chief priest.

"The parcel of foul plays has been untied," Ogbolu exclaimed. "The basket has covered the guilty ones."

* * * * * * *

A more vigorous search on their return in and around the compound led them nowhere.

'I just feel like scattering the chief priest's paraphernalia with my feet," Mazi Okwundu fumed.

"I've never trusted them one bit. Why can't he just mention the name or names of the culprits?" Mazi Ngwu wanted to know, if he knows. Why couldn't he just say where we can find her and spare the poor girl the pains of an untimely death. I doubt whether those greedy men see anything. If they do, either they don't see very well or they don't disclose all that they saw."

"Maybe they see all and very well too but since the coming of the white man, they've become afraid. No one knows what one would say to merit eating the white man's beans and wearing the derogatory dress one did sew by oneself. I don't blame them, the world is much more complex now than before. We don't know whose laws we are under now; whether it is our own native laws, that of the woman king or that of the church."

"Whichever it is," Arinze interrupted, "either the chief priest and other diviners say things definite or they pack up and we know we have no diviners any longer. These half measures do no one any good. We nearly lynched you by the wrong information we were given. Now the oracle wants us to believe she is held by one of our relatives. And, who should this be, Ogbuefi Udemba? He is the only Ichie we have here, Mazi Ngwu is not yet an Ichie. Let them stop planting seeds of discord in our unified family."

Mazi Ngwu opened his two palms wide in surprise.

"If I hadn't paid all the fees for the Ozo title, they would have said I kidnapped my brother's granddaughter for money. But God so kind, I've proved that I have enough money for me and my family for generations to come. Let nobody mention Ogbuefi Udemba's name here if you still want peace in this family. He just couldn't do it. I know my brothers." Mazi Ngwu suddenly folded his two arms across his chest, shrunk his frame, gazed up and lamented his fate. "My detractors have ruined my initiation ceremony."

"They can't succeed," Okwundu insisted. "You are more or less an Ichie now. Anyone who hopes to stop us is merely trying to mould a piece of cold metal."

Mazi Ngwu's heart skipped a beat when his brother mentioned his recognition as an Ichie. He subsequently felt relaxed at Okwundu's show of support.

They then decided to keep their eyes wide open while they waited till after the initiation ceremony the following day. It was hoped that she would be still alive by then and besides that her captors wouldn't risk transferring her during the festival when the entire compound would be teeming with people.

Where she lay Chinelo wept for the little progress her people have made in the wrong direction.

* * * * * *

"My brother, when will you learn to be sensible," Ogbolu's sister opened the attack immediately Ogbolu entered home.

"Udego," their father called her for restraint.

"You are calling me in vain," she replied. "I say you are calling me in vain because I will continue speaking until he hears. I know you people have tired of repeating the same much too frequently. I am not because if the palm kernel is not exhausted, the jaws will never rest." She then turned to Ogbolu who was avoiding the wrath of his second wife by staying dumb-founded in the parlour. "So, you are not afraid to visit Wamba land all alone despite the threatening message that stupid in-law of yours sent you?" she enquired.

Ogbolu frowned menacingly and opened his two palms to shield him from her foul word.

"Udego," her father repeated.

"Stop shouting my name this dead night but instead speak to your son. When I asked him not to marry Chinelo's mother, he defied me and you people supported him saying that a good wife was a good wife even if married from Utomkom. I agreed. When Nnenna couldn't give birth early enough, I advised you to remarry. You refused and our parents supported you. Our father even drove me away from his house," she broke down and sobbed.

"I did not drive you away," Ogbolu's father denied. 'I only asked you to go home to avoid trouble. I never drove my first daughter away from her first home."

"You people thought I was against anybody but didn't realise that I saw something before protesting. Now, I have asked him to marry a third wife when it has become apparent that his second may not give birth beyond her two children, all females. What do we do with females? And I have allowed him, believing that it isn't love but fear for his wives that makes him loathe the idea of a pair of wives."

"Udego," her father interrupted her. "This is the third time I am calling your name."

"Go on and call me. He dragged his feet on important issues yet, when the people of Inwelle wanted to lure him to his death, he sheepishly followed them. You are searching for Chinelo, a child that has brought you bad luck by preventing you from having children early and from having a boy. You are looking for Chinelo as if you don't know that the people over there make money charms with human beings. You are looking for Chinelo as if you expected to see her again when she went to live permanently with those people. They all conspired and sold her. And I am advising you to keep away from that girl unless you want to give your life. I'm saying this because I'm tired of wearing black dresses and jewels. Pity yourself my brother, pity yourself." She broke off and wept.

Where he sat, Ogbolu felt jinxed by the apparent hard truth. He loathed his senior sister's noisy and aggressive way of making her points on even very genuine cases as the present one. His resentment of her way of approach did not becloud the sense in what she was saying. He had taken an unnecessary risk but it was his own blood, Chinelo, that was pulling him.

"If I didn't go, they'll assume I was the culprit their confused oracle was referring," he pleaded in self-defence.

"And what did they say happened to her," a sober Udego asked.

"That she was being held in the compound by a titled man who is one of her fathers."

"And there are no titled men in their compound who match the description the oracle gave," Udego asked.

"There is but he seems to live above board," Ogbolu answered. "The oracle wasn't very definite."

"No oracle would ever be more explicit unless you want its grooves to be demolished by the white man. It is you people that have refused to face facts and accuse the actual person. Maybe they are afraid of the culprit or maybe they are all party to the plot and want to use you as a sacrificial lamb. I'll advise you not to go to that place again. Instead send somebody to go and inform your mischievous in-law that he knew the fact but only wanted to prevent the course of justice. Accuse him that he knew that one of his brothers was responsible and the truth will come out. Act tough and they'll know they are dealing with people who have brains as well. How I wished the white priest didn't destroy the Ajani oracle. It would have mentioned names. I have finished and I'm going," she stood up to go.

"Why not sleep here now that it has become very dark. The forces of evil are unleashed at this time of the day," her father suggested.

"I'll go. My children can't sleep without seeing me. Besides, I didn't inform my husband that I'll sleep away."

She tied her sleeping baby firmly on her back and made for the door. Her father wanted to escort her but Ogbolu dissuaded him but did it instead.

"Let them for once act like brothers and sisters," Ogbolu's father said.

"This is the first time our daughter had made herself as explicit as possible," his wife conceded.

"But she still has to curb her noisy tendencies," Ogbolu's father added.

"She'll die with it," his wife predicted, "if you ever hope on her turning into cold water tomorrow, you must be pouring water on dry rock. She'll have less opportunity of exhibiting her wildness when her brother starts acting more maturely and realistically."

"Woman," he called out, "mind your mouth. You would have told him when he was here but you acted the mute. You would have said this earlier," he advised as he stood up and left the room.

* * * * * *

Chinelo lay where they left her with pains trying to tear her little frame apart. She wondered how long she'll have to wait to find out why she was being held captive in her mother's uncle's house. She was no more hungry because her daily dose of watery pap was regular and adequate. She heard all that was said about her disappearance and hoped that her grandfather should trust his brothers less absolutely. She heard of the call for suspension of organised search for her until the Ozo initiation was over. She was confident that one of the numerous visitors, friends and relatives invited for the initiation, would stumble on her.

She had stopped crying for sometime now and waited with patient expectation that things would soon be alright. She, however, could not hide her feelings when the "Egwu Onwa" began. She heard the shrill voice of Nwogo singing the beckoning song to rally the play groups. Nwogo sang out the names of all the children in the vicinity and all the children present chorused for her! . . .

Onye aputaro,
Elim utala elilisie ya isi, elim utala
Onye aputaro,
Elim utala elilisie ya isi, elim utala;
Chinelo apuraro,
Elim utala, elilisie ya isi, elim utala; · · · · · ·

"Stop calling Chinelo," a voice advised Nwogo, "don't you know that she was kidnapped?"

"I didn't call her deliberately," she offered. "It was accidental. But, have they lost hope of finding her?"

"No, they just suspended the search till after the initiation," the voice answered.

"I thought they've abandoned the search. I wonder where she is now," Nwogo pursued, temporarily abandoning her primary assignment.

A grown-up ran out from Mazi Okwundu's house towards the children.

"Do what you are here for and don't stay here and gossip about Chinelo. You are too small to discuss the things of the elders. Besides, what you are saying is reviving sad memories in people. Can't you hear people crying? Okay! Nwogo, start singing, sing loud for we don't seem to hear you well but avoid the use of Chinelo's name, she'll join you but not now."

The children took her advice and set about their plays and singing in praise of the wealth and kindness of Mazi Ngwu.

Where she lay, Chinelo could not hold back the tears but still hoped. She felt cheated at being kept away from the "Egwu onwa" for which she had prepared very seriously. She heard all that the children said and had some inspiration from the promise of the elder who spoke to the children to the effect that she'll soon be free.

She was not the only one who felt the pang of pain at the song and subsequent discussions of the playing children. Mazi Okwundu heard well and clear. If he were not a man, he would have wept as Ogonna did. He shook his head violently to drive away the instinct to breakdown and with his head in his hands, reviewed all the recent occurrences. He drew a blank when he tried desperately to locate any area where they hadn't ransacked in search of Chinelo. He thought of what he'll tell the Guru people if he failed to locate Chinelo. He even thought of all the possible things Chinelo's captors could use her for, the possible agonies she could pass and the general state of despondency. He was mad at his abyssmal failure and took temporary solace in a keg of palm wine and his box of snuff both of which he consumed in alarming quantities while he waited impatiently for the embarrassing Ozo initiation to be over.

* * * * * *

The "Egwu onwa" continued uninterrupted with the family's

problem buried temporarily and shallowly in the dust raised by the feet of the playing children. Despite the fact that it was rainy season, the rain makers did their work well up till that "Egwu onwa" period. The weather had been dry for the previous two days and the entire village praised Mazi Ngwu for his ability to buy off the rain. In addition, though it was the period for the Umuafor festival, the blood chilling voice of the night tiger spirits were not heard even in a whisper. Mazi Ngwu had seen to that as well. He had pleaded with the young boys who had been initiated into manhood. These boys, who swept the village square, took one shilling and promised to inform the tiger spirit of Ngwu's desire that the spirits appearance for that night be delayed till sometime a little beyond midnight. It seemed that the tiger spirit accepted the offer because by midnight the "Egwu onwa" group was still having a merry good time. Occasionally, a group of the square sweepers would enter the playground to see the extension of play. They played around with the other children before disappearing once more.

Meanwhile, the "Egwu onwa" continued unabated. Mazi Ngwu's children and sisters sang and danced round in the crowd boasting of their fathers' and brothers' wealth and magnanimity of heart. Occasionally, Mazi Ngwu, who basked in the false glory of the praises and flattery, came down from a raised platform to spray small denomination of coins on his praise singers. This attracted more praises and boosted the morale of the playing group. Neighbours and invited guests, who intended to sleep over, called him his title name over cups of palm wine and local gin. Everything went smoothly for all except the village square boys who on their last visit discovered that the organisers of the "Egwu onwa" had no intention of honouring the promise made to them. They left the playground fuming and before they got to the Idemili groove, the first tiger spirit roared in protest. By the time Ngwu's emissary could arrive with a two shilling peace money, the other tiger spirits had taken over in annoyance. The entire village reverberated in their sound. The playground became ice-cold as the children and ladies dispersed despite Ngwu's assurance that the spirits wouldn't come near the playground. The frightened children believed him but could not resist the fear-instilling voice of thunder that seem to be coming nearer and nearer only to move away.

The older people stayed put for sometime before they were driven in by heavy wind.

"They are driving away any trace of rain that is in the sky and capable of disturbing us tomorrow," Ogbuefi Udemba suggested.

"Yes," agreed Ngwu. "I employed the best of the rain makers in this village and the neighbouring villages. No single rain will drop on this soil for the next two days," he boasted.

He had barely finished and Ogbuefi Udemba was half way praising him when an exceptionally powerful wind brought with it a small but significant amount of rain drops which made their debut with the soil.

Mazi Ngwu looked at Ogbuefi Udemba who stared back.

"This is not rain but dew of blessings from above," Mazi Ngwu propounded.

He had hardly finished when the second wave of large drops of rain arrived.

"Izundu," Ngwu yelled, "run down to Mazi Ojadi, the rain maker and ask him what is really happening."

Before Izundu could leave, the rain came in earnest and the accompanying wind tore down virtually everything on its path. Izundu defied the rain as he made his way to the rain maker's house. He was already out of the compound when he heard the crashing sound in the direction of the back of the compound. He didn't wait to find out but ran on.

A lot of people were speaking and thanking God at the same time when he came back. The rain still continued with undiminished intensity but people defied it to go and watch the miraculous work of God.

Izundu proceeded to the site of activity to discover that a large palm tree had fallen. It missed the house of Mazi Okwundu and that of his brother, Mazi Ngwu but, smashed down a greater portion of the wall of Ngwus "Ofe".

"What did he say," demanded a fuming and embarrased Ngwu.

"He said that the atmosphere was too heavy with rain so he had to release some of it so as to ensure a rain-free day tomorrow. He said he did it deliberately and in good faith. That you shouldn't worry, because he timed it so as not to disturb the "Egwu Onwa".

"What did I tell you," Ogbuefi Udemba demanded. "I knew the atmosphere was heavy with rain so the best thing to do was to release some at convenient period."

Mazi Ngwu shook violently throughout the night as the thought of recent occurrences drove sleep several miles away from his eyes. He regretted getting involved in all that mess. He hated the idea of continuing with his exploits but lacked both the physical and will powers to turn back the hand of time which has passed beyond a point of no return.

It was still raining, though less seriously, by the following morning when the initiation was due. Young men set on the fallen palm tree and before the first cock crow, it had been chopped up and cleared. Underneath the debris was a young royal python that the fallen tree had killed beside Mazi Ngwu's carved idols. A quick look at it, Ngwu's demeanor changed for the worst as he rightly interpreted that the oracle was quite aware of what he did and had declared it an abomination for which the gods should be adequately appeased or they run amuck with bows and arrows. The futility of his actions dawned on him. He couldn't stop his initiation into the Ozo title as much as he could not release Chinelo. Worse still, he dared not consult the oracle to find out how he would appease the gods of the land. But that would entail self-confession which he couldn't do. He thought of committing suicide but concluded that it would only create more problems especially for his family. Instead, he preferred to sit in and dare all consequences.

* * * * * *

The "Ufie", the Ozo special talking drum could be heard intermittently a few meters away from Mazi Ngwu's compound as it battled its way to be heard above the incessant clatter of the "dew of blessing from above." It was played from the side of Mazi Ngwu's house which was the best accommodation its player could find as he shied away from rain. He only came to the shade prepared for the Ichies on few occasions when the rain subsided enough to give the ceremony a lease of life.

Mazi Ngwu's friends, relatives and other guests spent most of their time indoors in several houses. The Ichies, themselves, fumed and cursed Ngwu for not consulting the good rain makers. They performed most of the rites inside Mazi Ngwu's house. The rain only gave him time to embrace his wife publicly thrice as demanded by custom. Thereafter, they hurriedly tied two cord strings around his ankles and donned his head with a red cap. But, they didn't forget to extract their fine of two guineas from him for allowing rain to beat them which was a great insult.

The rain, despite the fact that it wetted the gun powder and canon which were set ready for use early in the morning, didn't prevent the hosts from preparing food for the Ichies. All the small spaces in all the houses in the vicinity were used for this end. Other guests didn't see the smoke let alone the food that were prepared by them. Everyone agreed that it was the worst initiation ceremony in living history but some attributed the rain and its consequent destruction to the handiwork of enemies who Ogbuefi Otue Omee had underrated.

Where he sat, Ogbuefi Otue Omee sat shocked over the unexpected severity of the anger of the gods. He tactfully avoided the searching eyes of people. He knew the real cause of his calamity and wondered the extent to which the gods would carry their anger. He looked gloomy and waited impatiently for the ceremonies to be over.

Ogbuefi Udemba sat by his side and kept on giving him words of encouragement which were obviously misdirected.

Mazi Okwundu and his household were not in attendance having excused themselves for obvious reasons. Throughout the ceremonies, Mazi Okwundu's thoughts strayed wide as he tried to pin Chinelo's abduction on somebody. He found it difficult to suspect Ogbuefi Udemba even though the oracle would have borne him in mind while describing the culprit. But recent incidences in Ogbuefi Otue Omee's house was really a food for thought for him. The rain, the fallen tree and the death of the royal python were all pointers to the fact that the gods were annoyed. But to whom? The calamities could either mean that the gods were annoyed with the entire family or against the single individual being afflicted. He then painfully went through the evidences presented to him and more especially, those from the chief priest. He then concluded that Ogbuefi Otue Omee might not be absolutely absolved. He decided to consult another oracle early the next day. He wanted to hear from a different source altogether so as to avoid bias. He was still contemplating on which oracle to visit when Ogbolu's emissary arrived.

"Ogbolu said that the oracle at Isinka told him this." Mazi Okwundu asked unbelievingly.

"Yes and that she may never be found again," the messenger included.

"Arinze," Mazi Okwundu called out. "Let somebody call me Arinze and Chigbata."

"My good friend, kindly repeat your story," Okwundu begged the man from Guru immediately Arinze and Chigbata took their seats. "Don't be annoyed that you have been asked to repeat the same story again. I just want them to hear with their own ears. You are aware that a snake killed by a single individual has a mysterious way of turning into a royal python. Bear with me."

"There is no harm at all. Ogbuefi Ogbolu went to the oracle at Isinka and was told that the girl was abducted by one of his grandfathers who used the money to initiate into the ozo title. Worse still was that the girl may never be seen again."

"I don't believe," said Arinze, "after all, Ogbuefi Otue Omee had paid all the Ozo money before Chinelo got missing."

"And another thing is that our oracle had maintained that she was still within the compound up till yesterday. So, she wouldn't have been sold for the Ozo title," Chigbata added.

"Which one do I follow now?" Okwundu asked dejectedly. "One oracle said that she is held by one of my brothers only to say that she doesn't know those people holding her. Which of my brothers wouldn't Chinelo know? Except the dead ones. One said the captor is a titled man of medium age. The only titled man in our family is above seventy years. And now, the oracle of Isinka has come with this absurd information that Ngwu used the money he collected from selling her to initiate into the Ozo society even though we are aware that he had finished all major payments before her disappearance. Which one do we follow? Go tell Ogbolu that I've got his message and would be consulting a different oracle for confirmation. Tell him that I'll be informing him on the outcome later."

"I'm fed up with these oracles," he complained. "Call names, they won't but only cast a thick cloud over a whole village in trying to isolate an individual. When I get there tomorrow, I'll ask the Chief Priest point blank questions. Call me Egwu when you get back," he asked of

Arinze.

"One thing is knowing the person, another is the accused accepting that he did it. This case is becoming very complex and dangerous. We shall proceed cautiously so as not to trigger an irreparable family split," Chigbata pleaded as he made for his house.

"My son," Okwundu said when Egwuonwu made his presence known. "You look so clumsy this evening. Are you well at all?"

"I am hungry," Egwuonwu complained.

"Our town's woman," Okwundu called Unaku, his wife, "Kindly bring this boy some food. His breath is too shallow." Then turning again to Egwuonwu, he continued. "After eating, my son, you'll run an errand for me. You'll run fast to Obogwu village and inform Ogbuefi Odonsi that I'll be calling on him first thing in the morning. If he asks you why, tell him you don't know. Do you hear?"

Egwuonwu nodded as he gozzled a plateful of boiled yam and vegetables in palm oil.

"You know his house well?"

Egwuonwu nodded again.

"And remember you must run fast so that you'll be back quick. It doesn't seem as if the rain is satisfied yet."

"Ehee," Egwuonwu responded. After polishing the small porter in which the lunch/dinner was supplied, cleaned his hand on the sole of his left foot, he dashed off in the direction of Obogwu.

"Good child," Okwundu complimented, "Fast," he reminded him.

* * * * * *

Egwuonwu was still delivering his message to a tipsy Ogbuefi Odonsi when the heavens yawned again. "Today's rain frightens me," Odonsi informed the small boy who was embarrassed to enter into an informal discussion with the old fame native doctor. He didn't know what to say so he characteristically nodded.

"I've never seen such rains in my life," he continued ignorant of the fast breathing and shaky legs of the errand boy. "Ehe, you said your father said he'll be coming here first thing tomorrow morning? And you don't know why? Ok, tell him I'll be in. Though I have a little work to do for some people at Idagbe tomorrow morning but not all that early. Tell your father that I got his message and will be ready for him. But you should stay behind until the rain has lessened."

Egwuonwu waited for hours for the rain to stop. By the time the heavens signified with lightning and thunders that it was satisfied, it was already pitch dark.

Ogbuefi Odonsi produced his short, smooth and naturally sculptured "Ofo" stick. He struck Egwuonwu gently with it first on his forehead and then on top of each of his feet.

"Go on my son," he yelled at the top of his voice, "neither man nor demon can harm you. Don't fear. I have them where I want them." He patted Egwuonwu's head as he urged him on to go.

Armed with the assurance of Odonsi, Egwuonwu braved the darkness, lightnings, thunders, kidnappers, head hunters and the numerous evil spirits that were let loose that night and raced down the road to his village.

He was climbing up the small hill that eventually bowed to the overwhelming magnitude of a subsequent valley when suddenly, his body shivered and all the courage left him. He stopped on his track. He didn't know what he was afraid of but a benevolent lightning soon showed him. A large pregnant royal python was lying across the road a few meters from his feet.

Egwuonwu screamed and ran back. He kept on jumping up as he saw millions of imaginary royal pythons littering his path. He was still running when one hunter appeared from the bush some distance up his way. Egwuonwu would have died of fright when he heard the voice except that he saw the hunters light a long way off.

"What is it my son?" the hunter asked when his light picked up the small boy.

"A boa constrictor," answered Egwuonwu as he gasped for air.

"Where?"

"Up there," Egwuonwu answered pointing up the road.

"Come and show me," the hunter nudged him along.

The hunter's powerful light picked up the comparatively small reptile when the two night travellers were still a long way off.

"It is not a boa constrictor but a royal python," the hunter corrected. "But this one is large and pregnant. This is the first time I'm seeing a pregnant royal python. Come, let me escort you pass it."

The two walked towards the python which stood its ground.

"By the way, whose son are you?" the hunter asked.

Egwuonwu told him.

"Your grandfather, Mazi Okwundu is my father's good friend. Tell your fathers not to be sending children out in the night. The night is very "deep" and full of mysteries," the hunter philosophised.

Egwuonwu, who was hiding closely on the side of the hunter, opposite the python, was so shaken with fright that he didn't remember to tell the hunter that he left home early but was kept behind by rain.

The hunter escorted Egwuonwu over the other side of the road and came back to inspect the royal python more closely before passing back into the wet bush.

Egwuonwu continued feverishly on his interrupted journey home. His teeth were rattling seriously as he passively descended the valley.

He was directly adjacent to the monstrous Iroko tree at the bottom of the valley when lightning showed the danger; a thickly mustached man was standing directly on his path barely a meter away from him. He had his sharp matchet raised threateningly and ready to descend.

"Nnam OO!" Egwuonwu shouted as he tried to cow away but he didn't move so fast.

"Whaam," the matchet landed on his shoulder with its side. "Tell your father never to send you out at night again. I'm leaving you because of an old friendship. Run home."

Egwuonwu lay where he fell and decades passed before he found his breath. He rose slowly and felt his shoulder where he was hit. It was painful. He heard some discussion at the foot of the Iroko to know that his assailants were still near. That revamped his sense of danger. He ran and never stopped till he met his grandfather, Okwundu and his father Arinze walking fast in search for him.

"What type of temptation has come to our family this period. Let God take away the power of the devil. My son, lets go," Okwundu said as he lifted the boy on to his shoulder and they went home.

"We must be very careful," Arinze cautioned, "the devil wants something from our body. But after washing its hand, it would only soil it again by resting them on the ground, not on any one of us."

"Did you fall down?" Okwundu asked as drops of sand kept on

falling on his face.

"One man hit me down with the side of his matchet," Egwuonwu answered.

"Where?" an alarmed Okwundu asked.

"At the Iroko tree down the road."

"Who?"

"I didn't see him well but he has a thick set of dirty moustach."

"Ogbuefi Ichele," Okwundu exclaimed. "So, he could do this to my own son?".

"He said he was leaving me because of an ancient friendship and that you should learn not to be sending your children out at night."

"I wonder why Ogbuefi Odonsi allowed you to go without escort," Okwundu wondered.

"He rubbed his "Ofo" stick on my forehead and legs and said that I shouldn't fear because nothing would harm me."

"I know he is good at his trade. But, even if his art could protect you from absolute death, it wouldn't stop somebody from hitting you as has just happened. I don't like this over confidence in our native doctors. 'Nothing would happen,' They'll tell you but at last, something does happen and they shift the blame either to you, your personal god or your enemies. As if they didn't know these things existed before they did their prediction. I hope he didn't hit you hard," Okwundu suggested.

"No," answered Egwuonwu impulsively though the searing pain on his right shoulder seemed to tell a different story. Mazi Okwundu, Arinze and their households heard this more reliable story when light at home revealed the deep cut on Egwuonwu's shoulder.

"This Chinelo's case has ceased to be a joke," Okwundu noted with dismay.

"There is a deadly snake in the thatched roof. We are being tempted seriously so everybody should be extra careful from now on. My son, Ndo."

Ogbuefi Odonsi performed his opening rites quietly and with all ease. He took all the pieces of stick that represented each member of their entire household, straightened them well and tied them into a bunch. He passed the bunch over his oracle and finally dipped one end of the bunch into his big mortar of coloured water. He observed the bunch and the red coloured water closely. Then he started seeing invisible things and events.

"Who has the wrapper that is being eaten by a goat?" he asked the bewildered Okwundu, Arinze and Chigbata". "The head of the he-goat has fallen into the bag of the he-goat. The goat belonging to the tortoise has eaten the okro fruits belonging to the tortoise. She has been taken away. You, Okwundu, will never find her by your strength. It's all a wasted exercise. Don't mourn her and don't pursue the case any longer. I will not speak further."

"No, but who took her away?" a tired Okwundu asked.

"That is what you should avoid probing. It will create more problems than solving one. The truth will be heard when the time comes."

"So, what do you advise me to do now?" Okwundu asked.

"Nothing."

"What do I tell her father?"

"He won't ask you anything again unless you go to him."

"So you advise that we keep quiet."

"Yes and be patient. Things would work out themselves."

Okwundu and his two sons went back home not very sure who was insane: they themselves or the native doctor. After a frantic search and enquiries in towns, far and near, they came to the conclusion that Ogbuefi Odonsi was, as always, very sane.

* * * * * *

The 'Egwu Onwa' had barely been dispersed by the night tiger masquerade when the two men entered into the 'Ofe'. Chinelo thought her captivity was over.

"It is time," one of the men announced.

"I'd better go over the fence so that you hand her over to me. But, we must tie her up first." The other suggested.

Chinelo froze on realising that most probably, her ordeal was only beginning. She started weeping when they placed her in the over-sized wooden basket used in carrying yams and wood. They bound her firmly to the basket and covered her over with large banana leaves.

Both men carried the basket on to the top of the "Ofe" wall. One held it to keep it from falling while the other climbed the wall to the farm at the other side. The man in the farm held the basket in place while the second man climbed the wall. Together, they brought the basket down on to the head of one of them. They went through the farm towards the road leading to the community farm.

They were still within the farm when the palm tree fell but didn't stop to find out what happened. On the contrary, they hurried on to leave that vicinity at the shortest possible time.

On getting near the road, they discovered that the village square sweepers and their furiously threatening tiger spirits were amassed near their emergence point. The second man not carrying the basket ran on forward while the heavy laden man took the rear.

"Tiger spirit calm down," the scout shouted at the top of his voice. "I am with an "Ogbodu.""

Despite the noise, both the tiger spirits and their followers, the village square sweepers, heard the intruder loud and clear. For, all of a sudden, the tiger spirits held their peace and a deadening golden silence descended on the entire village and the environs. The tiger spirits speedily disappeared into the adjoining bushes and side roads. Their followers hastened to make a comfortable distance from the source of the approaching intruders, whose footsteps could be heard a long way off as their soles crushed the vegetation as they cautiously made for the road. And, had it not been for this noise, the tiger spirits, their followers, the intruders and maybe the entire village and its environs would have heard Ngwu grating his teeth as he wondered silently whether he wasn't insane to have gone so far into this abominable mess.

The men and the lady eventually emerged from the farm with the lady still air-borne. The only thing they saw was a group of young boys wandering about aimlessly in all directions like a colony of termites whose ant hill had been demolished by an overzealous farmer. Some of the boys made U-turns and came back to walk past the intruders. The spies were surprised to observe no lady among the entourage and had to conclude that the "Ogbodu" in question was not a woman but rather, one of the men and most probably, the man behind with a big load on his head. The young boys were not suspicious of the group because the very next day was the Ozo day for Mazi Ngwu and the Umuafor festival was equally at hand. Large masquerades could feature on both occasions, night masquerades could also feature. Gifts, in addition, moved both ways. So, no movement was suspicious under such circumstances. More importantly, they were more concerned with their tiger spirits than with anything and were too impatient to wait for the men to make a comfortable distance from them.

The two men and their load were hardly out of sight when the tiger Spirits roared into life once more.

"Vooh, Vooh, Vooh, Vooh, O O," they roared as they challenged, though belatedly, whoever was it that interrupted their sweet disturbance of the peace and sleep of the entire village.

The two men were happy when they made the large community farms on the outskirts of the village. They managed to shake hands on overcoming the first obstacle of the two they hoped to encounter. The second obstacle, the night hunters, who paraded the large dark wilderness called the farms, could be a serious embarrassment but the men were prepared.

* * * * * *

Kwasie, the hunter, tailed a group of grass cutters to a patch of elephant grass. He then lit the torch-light he was carrying on his head. The sudden change of visibility rattled the clever grass cutters and they quickly dashed off in a group for safer grounds. Kwasie was very disappointed but being a patient experienced hunter, traced them to their new foraging ground. He pointed his torch away from them before lighting it and then slowly turned it to their direction. The trick nearly worked except that during the turn, his gun collided with a tall elephant grass. A large shower of rain drops then fell loudly on the plants and animals below. The animals, sensing serious danger, made off once more for the first patch of elephant grass. Kwasie shook his head.

"Today na today," he murmured as he slowly but stealthily went after them. This time, he decided to approach the elephant grass patch from the rear where the large water stones would afford him the cover he so much needed.

He had just rounded the palm tree on the farm path when he heard the sound. It was the sound of the rattler.

"Where on earth is this night masquerade going tonight?" he asked himself with the popular understanding that only dangerous masquerades use the rattler.

He stopped and listened to find out the way the masquerades was going. To his surprise, the sound became louder and louder. Kwasie edged himself into the bush but was doing it so slowly so as not to disturb the grasscutters he was tailing. Then, he heard the voice.

"The shadow that resembles a human being, are you on the move or are you lying in wait for me?" the leader among the two men asked in a voice similar to that of a masquerade.

He had been saying similar things ever since they approached the village farms. But that was the first one Kwasie heard and thought that the masquerade had spotted him from miles off.

"Is that a threat?" the voice asked again as if it saw Kwasie by means of one of the numerous charms allegedly possessed by night masquerades.

Kwasie, as far as he was concerned, knew he wasn't a threat except to the grass-cutters. He didn't wait to answer but when he discovered that the "masquerade" was gaining on him temporarily forgot about the grass-cutters and burst into a run. He didn't go far before he collided with one of the water stones that abound in the farm. He fell head-long, managed to rise quickly and, leaving his torch light and gun where each fell, ran on into the farm until he was sure he was safe enough. He ultimately found a big stone. Sat down and rubbed his left leg frantically in order to soothe the pains rising from one of his broken toes. From his rest position, he could hear the fading sound of the rattler and knew he had successfully avoided a serious danger though the broken tow was a source of another discontent.

The two men and their load continued undisturbed on their perilous journey to the big river not too sure what would chance. They were ignorant of the predicaments of Kwasie, the hunter, but held their hearts in their hands until they were far midstream with their illegal cargo. It was only when they passed the land of the illicit gin people, that the men felt safe enough to unbound her. Thereafter, they showed her a lot of pity but Chinelo was not deceived as she knew she was beyond the point of return. She likened her captors' show of pity to the one shown by a butcher to a cow under slaughter.

She was aware she was going on a long journey and wasn't quite sure that she would come back alive. Her condition was hopeless. She didn't know where they were or where they were going. She wanted to cry but the pains from her previously gagged mouth determined a limit for her expression of grief. She sobbed herself into sleep.

By the time she woke, the canoe had passed the land of the coconut people. At that point in time, her cousin, Egwuonwu, was busy delivering Mazi Okwundu's message to Ogbuefi Odonsi. And by the time her grandfather and uncles were at Odonsi's house the following morning, she had passed the land of the snail people and steadily heading for the slave market at Abanito.

Five days later, she was seated quietly in the large house of her new owner amidst half a dozen other newly bought slaves. She had bathed, combed and some of her previous radiance had started to show but she was far from being happy. But her unhappiness could not be compared with that at Inwelle where the search had ended abruptly. There was a sense of gloom everywhere which couldn't even be lifted by the arrival of new baby boy to the family. But the atmosphere of grief couldn't prevent the baby from receiving a name. So, when Chigbata's wife handed the smiling baby to Mazi Okwundu, he lifted him to his face.

"I wish you had come at a period of joy. But we are grieving. Your birth is therefore, a land mark for us. So, we shall call you Ifeatu (A thing of reference). But two names do not kill a man. So, in addition, we shall call you Agubamba, because, if the names of all the places we've gone in search of your sister, our daughter, Chinelo, are counted, the jaw will break in the process; the places are simply innumerable. Welcome, my son."

He handed the baby back to the mother, poured libations, took a cup of wine and the solemn occasion was through.

* * * * * *

No one had ever seen the wind, neither you nor I but when the trees bow down their heads, everyone knows that the wind is passing bye. So, when Mazi Alapa, the slave trader, breezed into the compound and refused to acknowledge the greetings of all and sundry, his wife's inclusive, it was very apparent that he wasn't in his best of moods. He had every cause to be annoyed because he had just been to the market and unfortunately, his customers didn't bring him enough goods to warrant a profitable journey to the main slave market at Dambata. He raved from one end of the compound to the other with his horse whip at the ready. He ordered that a couple of slaves be lashed severely for a couple of flimsy reasons. Fortunately, the youngest of the slave was not among the unlucky ones; she swept her own portion of the compound as thoroughly as was possbile. She equally scrubbed the master's sitting room so perfectly, that one could use it for a mirror. That, however, didn't prevent the master, Mazi Alapa, from finding faults in the work. He had to rescind an order that whoever was the worker should be flogged when the worker turned out to be Chinelo. She was already in tears when she was brought before the whip man.

"I can see that this group of people are Europeans who don't eat much of solid food. They would have told me early enough so that I'll be preparing "hot water" (tea) for them instead of throwing away large food remains all over the place," he complained.

Some of the slaves that heard him were surprised because they've never had enough to eat and, therefore, had none to waste unless as urine. They wondered silently where their master saw the wasted food in reference.

"And for that reason, their meals should be restricted to two times a day, one in the morning and another in the evening. That notwithstanding, each meal should be half of its present quantity. I need not mention that each should continue to do his or her normal daily chores."

He presently romped into his private compound where later cries and raised voices indicated that Mazi Alapa was carrying his annoyance to his family.

Mazi Alapa's annoyance failed to solve his basic problem. Though venting his spleen on his defenceless slaves saved him some ulcer and headache, and his austerity measure saved him some money, none saved him the time that was the bone of contentions; he still had to wait another seven days before he is prepared for Dambata main market.

The atmosphere in the slave camp was grievous thourhgout that evening. Most of the slaves sat or walked about dismayed and sad, not knowing for sure what fate had befallen them. Only one light illuminated the dark and damp cave, the voice of Chinelo. With tears still in her eyes, she sang one native song after another while she cracked palm kernels with a pair of stones and ate the seeds. She was so absorbed in what she was doing that she didn't observe that the entire inmates of the camp had fallen silent as they absorbed the balm of her song. And could she sing? She took after her mother, Nnenna, in that. Her suffering had only weakened her flesh and sharpened her voice and composure. She continued her hobby unabated until darkness descended on that part of the world. Chinelo reluctantly rose up, packed her stones neatly in a corner of the house. Sighs of disappointment escaped the mouths of more that half of the slaves when Chinelo stopped singing. They resisted a strong urge to ask her to continue.

"There is no need for us to kill ourselves here even before we are killed by our captors," Erewu a middle-aged mother from Inwelle advised. "One who is rejected by one's people does not have to reject oneself. We shall do something to enliven our spirits until the end comes. If it brings good, then we thank God. If, however, it brings bad, then we take it as fate. But for God's sake, let us do something before some of us go mad."

"And what do we do?" a young man's voice querried from one dark end. "Anything you suggest, I'll go along."

"I don't know from where you come from but in my own part of the world, when people have nothing doing, they sit down and tell stories to while away time. It will save us the boredom."

The other speaker sighed. Erewu thought it was in support of her suggestion but the poor boy thought she meant they should plan a way of escape.

"Go on," some one urged her, "start the stories. We are one everywhere; no sane fellow doesn't love good stories."

"No, I can't start. In my place, it is either the eldest or the youngest who starts folk stories. I am neither the eldest nor the youngest," Erewu, who was fast becoming the leader of the slaves ducked.

"We don't know who is the eldest here," another voice spoke, "because none of us was around when the other was born. Let the youngest start. I enjoyed her songs some minutes ago and wouldn't mind if she continues till day break."

They all then agreed that Chinelo should start. She willingly obliged.

* * * * * * *

"Once upon a time," she started cautiously after clearing her throat which didn't need clearing in the first place.

"And there was such a time," some people responded.

"But is that how people from your area start folk stories?" Erewu interrupted. "Don't they perform some rituals before that?"

"Then let me start from the beginning," Chinelo suggested.

"Ehe!" agreed her audience.

"Chaa Kpii," Chinelo heckled them.

"Woo." they responded.

"Chaa Kpii."

"Woo,"

"Otii," she continued.

"Oyoo," they answered back.

"O ha ni."

"O h a."

"Nkita nyara akpa."

"Nsi agwu n' ohia."

Then they all shouted in joy and happiness that all the Wambas had the same culture no matter the dialect.

"Once upon a time." she resumed.

"And there was such a time," her charged audience replied.

"There was a man and his wife. The man was a very good man and his wife was equally a good woman. They lived happily for several years without a baby. Both the man and woman were very sad and worried. But the woman was more worried than the husband because she loved the man so much and believed she owed him a baby. Her worries showed on her face and this distressed her husband who wouldn't like anything to disturb his beloved wife, not even the baby issue. He knew she was worried because of her inability to give him a baby.

'I've always told you not to worry about any baby', he admonished her. 'I am the one to worry but I don't because only God, in heaven, gives babies. His time is the best. No amount of worry can solve our problem. So, stop worrying, my good wife, and let us pray to God.'

His wife usually stopped worrying after such a sermon but she soon started all over again with time. At last, she couldn't bear the grief any longer so, she sneaked out one night to the native doctor who told her that any baby she delivered would take her life.

'Do you mean I'll ever conceive, that this my womb will ever carry a child but that the baby will take my life?', she asked the native doctor.

'Yes,' answered the native doctor solemnly.

'Only my life?' she repeated.

'Yes,' the native doctor replied.

'But the baby will live?' she asked.

'Yes,' he answered.

'That is fine. Life has no essence for me without a child. I just want my husband to have a baby of his own so that he becomes like other men. That is all.'

'But you'll die,' the native doctor reminded her.

'What does it matter? What use am I to him when he can't hold a baby! '

That did it. The native doctor asked her to repeat in four days time. When she still insisted on giving birth at the expense of her life, the native doctor reluctantly gave her some concoctions to open her womb.

One month after the visit, she became pregnant. She was very glad and her husband was glad as well. Nine months after the visit, she put to bed a bouncing baby girl. Throughout the period of pregnancy, she never betrayed any fear of death which was sure to come during or after delivery. That was a secret she shared with only the native doctor. She wasn't, therefore, surprised when death stole in even before she was able to carry the baby in her hands. But she smiled all the way to death because she was rest assured that her husband would be happy despite her death as she had proved him a man.

The man mourned his beloved wife until people thought he'll follow her there. But the love for the baby and good counsel prevailed and he lived. He loved his baby even more than he loved the mother.

He never allowed her to play with the other children and made her sleep on his stomach. She lacked nothing.

But as a man cannot live forever without a wife, he soon found himself another one whom he strongly instructed to take good care of the girl. The new wife readily agreed and kept to her promise. Both her and her husband showered love on the girl. But later, she got her own children and started taking more interest in their affairs and less in hers. She equally became jealous that her husband seemed to love this girl more than her own children. Consequently, she started to maltreat this girl. She was poorly fed and irregularly too.

Whenever her step-mother wanted to go to farm, she'll feed her children very well and her poorly. In addition, she'll keep their lunch in the lower rungs of the rafters over the fire place. But hers, she usually put in the higher rungs where her hands couldn't reach. Then came afternoon, this orphan would cry and sing to the dead mother telling her what her step-mother was doing to her. On each occasion, her mother would come from her grave laden with all types of delicious meals for the girl. She would then feed to her fill enough to last her a whole day. Consequently, the orphan was healthier than her step-brothers and sisters to her step-mother's surprise. Her father took her healthy look to mean that his second wife was treating her step-daughter very fine. But soon, his second wife started beating her step-daughter very often accusing her of either stealing pieces of meat or pieces of fish in her soup pot. She reprimanded her at the slightest provocation and no amount of persuasion from her husband could stop her. So, not surprisingly, the small girl became sickly, melancholic and developed a ghostly appearance. The girls mother saw all these from her grave and was highly pained. She decided that her co-wife should be taught a bitter lesson of a life time.

Not long thereafter, the man's second wife went to market and bought some star apple fruits. She gave one each to her children and none to her step-daughter. Her step-daughter stayed by the back of the house and wept as her step-brothers and sisters ate their star apple fruits. At this her moment of grief, her mother appeared to her and wiped off her tears. She was then instructed not to cry but to plant one of the seeds of the star apples later on that day. Her mother taught her the songs she'll be singing to hasten the growth of the tree. The orphan was much relieved before her mother left.

Later on, she planted the seed of the star apple in her father's farm. She sang one of the songs that her mother taught her and the seedling grew into a tree. She then sang the tree to produce fruits and it did. She then sang the fruits to ripen and fall and they did. She collected as many as she could carry and then asked the tree to return to the seed stage. The tree obeyed. She went home with the star apple fruits and shared them evenly with her step-mother, her step-brothers and sisters. They were surprised and enquired from where she got them but she didn't tell them.

She continued collecting fruits by this way until her step-mother decided to find the source of her step-daughter's fortnue.

That evening, her step-mother tailed her to the spot in her father's farm and observed the ritual with rapt attention. She would have left unnoticed except that she stepped on a centipede and shouted in alarm. Then she was spotted by the orphan. The orphan thought that the game was up but her mother appeared suddenly and told her what to do. She went home happy.

The very next day, her step-mother was at the spot. She sang the necessary songs and at the end, collected a basket-full of fruits. She wasn't satisfied with the quantity because it wasn't enough to be carried to market, so, she called her first son to climb the tree. Her first son got lost in the foliage of the tree but couldn't collect a single fruit. She lost patience with him and invited the second son. He also couldn't be of much help. So, she finally climbed herself.

When she was well up, the orphan emerged from her hiding place and rapidly sang that the tree should grow taller and taller. The tree obeyed and continued to grow until the top disappeared into the clouds. The people on top became frightened and asked for mercy.

Meanwhile, the sudden emergence of mammoth tree in the village attracted the entire village who asked what had happened, and were told. They blamed the woman on top of the tree for her wickedness and greed but asked the little girl to forgive them. She did and asked the tree to shorten into a seedling and then into a seed. The tree obeyed and the three people on top were salvaged.

From then on, the villagers respected the girl and all orphans, for that matter. Besides, the girl's step-mother treated her like a small goddess and there was peace. This story teaches that it isn't good for anyone to maltreat orphans because a tailless cow has its god to drive away flies for it. Chaa Kpii, Chaa Kpii," she heckled then in counclusion but to her surprise, she got no reply.

Erewu and a couple of others were in tears. Erewa because the thought of her children and what their step-mother would be doing to them had occurred to her.

"If I had known I'll be a source of renewed sorrow to you, I would have told another story," Chinelo said remorsefully.

"Chinelo," Erewu called out suddenly amidst tears, "are you the daughter of Nnenna, the first daughter of Mazi Okwundu of Inwelle?"

"Yes, and who are you? Are you from our area?"

Chinelo never got an answer because Erewu was in a hysterical mood as the events that culminated in her unscheduled journey to Izombe unfolded to her like a coloured film.

* * * * * *

Erewu left home early that morning as most traders do. She managed to wash her face before she left and hurriedly swallowed three or four lumps of cold pounded cassava with cold egusi soup in between her hurried preparation. She was still having last lump when the last cock crowed and she knew it was time to move. As she moved to their carved wooden door, she gave instructions to her junior sister, who was living with her, on how to keep her home while she was away.

"I'll be back just before sun set," she informed Usoku. "Make sure you people feed very well and make sure your father is served well. He'll give you yam for afternoon meals. You know how to prepare it. The fermented oil bean seed is in the basket. Be merciful to both salt and pepper. You know that our father does not take plenty of pepper. Eheee! Before I forget, collect some bitter leaf, spread them in the sun and make sure they wilted well. Wash them properly and keep for me. Boil and pound for me an equivalent amount of cocoyam. Let it not have lumps. I'll bring back fish for the soup. Look after the house well and make sure the children are well bathed."

"Naa Gboo," Usoku wished her. "Buy elele and akara."

"Alright, I'll soon be back," Erewu promised and hurried on her way to join the stream of traders going down to Guru daily market.

Usoku waved at her until she was out of sight.

Despite Usoku's good wishes and waves, business was a disaster for Erewu that day. In fact, it was the worst market day in all her business life. There was simply no fish in the market for her to buy. None of her Aboki customers was at the Guru market. It then occurred to her that her customer's had previously informed her of a fast approaching yearly religious festival which could keep them from market for some days.

"I can't just go back to Inwelle empty-handed," she vowed. "If only I can see Igbo-ada-aka fish, I could manage with that until this bad weather passes away."

Then she heard a man laughing as loudly as was possible without flies making nests in one's mouth.

"The market is not as bad," the man informed her. "There are good fish but it depends on whether you have the money," he informed her as he wiped tears from his eyes.

"Let me see the basket of fish first. Leave the money issue," she promised.

"The fish is there," the man promised. "Even if you want ten baskets, you'll have them," he promised, "but your purse must be heavy."

"Show me the fish first," Erewu dared him.

"You doubt a lot. So, you don't know me, your in-law. I just want to make you rich as an in-law, otherwise, I would have sold it off a long time ago. In addition, I'm new to this trade and so, I'll like to make customers."

"I can see with you but how can I price what I didn't see? In-law, business is business. That is why a mother and her child still do business."

"Alright," agreed the man and went into the house.

He soon re-emerged with a heavy basket of dried fish and a didn't-I-tell-you smile. He carefully removed the papers and jute bag covering the fish to expose the largest and best types of fish one could possibly see in that market. Erewu shrugged and came nearer.

"These ones are too large. No one may be able to buy them in our local markets. But what is the price anyway?"

"They are costly," came the reply.

"As costly as what?"

"Six shillings."

"Erewu looked the man seriously on the face and looked away.

"Obviously," she thought, "this man is a new man in this trade otherwise he would have known that worse baskets of fish sell even better than that."

"Would you sell them to me at five shillings?" she asked.

"That is why I hate this pricing system. There is never a time people believe that a said price is nice," he complained. "My last price is five and six. Would you buy or not?"

"We are not quarrelling, my in-law. This is trade. Anybody is free to price anything."

"That does not mean you'll start pricing my fish what the vulture prices the corpse. I 'dashed' you the fish. Go and enjoy the profit. Only remember to come back and tell me how you fared."

"Don't you have smaller fishes?" she asked as she counted out money for four baskets of fish.

"I have them but they are not here, they are at the island. I'll go directly and bring them."

The kind man then hurried off towards the river bank.

"Madam, it is better for you to follow 'oga' to the island otherwise, he may forget you are here and may even sell the fish to someone else not necessarily at a higher price," the man's apprentice helping hand wisely advised Erewu "God just gave you this fish."

Erewa needed no more urging but followed the man towards the river bank.

She got to the island quite alright but the return journey wasn't as straightforward. It was the return journey that brought Erewu on her long, painful and unscheduled journey to Izombe with neither fish nor her money. Worse still, her freedom was no more in her own hands. It was agonising, more so at that moment when the innocent girl for whom the people of Guru had kidnapped her in revenge had vividly painted a true picture of the agonies of children without mothers.

Erewu wept and others followed suit but each for slightly different reasons.

From his living quarters, Mazi Alapa inclined his ear in the direction of the slave house. He heard no sound escept the low murmur of a single voice. Then, he suspected that most probably, the slaves were having a meeting and may be planning their escape. He beckoned three of his hench men and asked them to escort him to the slave house.

As they came closer, the murmur turned into a mesmerising, treble, high-pitched voice of Chinelo as she meandered her way through the intricate story with the expertise of a veteran. They were captivated and listened attentively to the end. They were moved beyond description but they didn't enter. They stayed out the subsequent discussion. They went back to their living quarters as dejected as the slaves.

"That is why I don't go near them very often. And when I do, I'm always harsh," Mazi Alapa confessed. "If you form the habit of listening to them, you won't ever take one to the next market. Soft hearts don't do this business. It is a man's job."

"But Oga, this girl has a voice," one of his henchmen confessed.

"She is a dish which must not be used to carry ash. We shall see what we shall do about her case. But, if you ever want to be successful in this business, never listen to your slaves unless you are speaking to them simultaneously with a whip."

* * * * * *

A month later, Chinelo had finished sweeping the compound and was busy scrubbing one of the houses when her master, Mazi Alapa woke from sleep. He listened to the song and the voice. They didn't belong to this world but they belonged to Chinelo. He didn't then regret his decision not to sell Chinelo with the others. On the contrary, he even wished she wasn't a slave so that he would marry her. It would be very demeaning for him to marry a slave, no matter her beauty, worth or the circumstances. He tried to locate her town but decided against such a move as that may result in her owners claiming her back. Besides, Chinelo knew only the name of Inwelle but not the route. She never remembered she was not from Inwelle but from Guru. Mazi Alapa had never heard of Inwelle and never knew such a town existed. He would have been able to trace her home if she had mentioned Guru for Mazi Alapa knew Guru very well as a major slave

104

source.

* * * * * *

Time and opportunities later proved that Chinelo was an asset and a highly talented lady indeed. She became loved by all the villagers but each shrugged when the fact that she was a slave was remembered. She soon became part of Mazi Alapa's family and at a time acted as his first born. Whenever the husband and wife were to be away at the same time, all the household was handed over to her. She acted well in that capacity. She, time without number, acted as an unofficial wife of Mazi Alapa, preparing meals, going to market, leading other slaves to farm and general organisation. She even taught the villagers new types of preparing meals. One of the meals she introduced was moi moi. This earned her the name of "Ada elele" (moi moi girl).

But age soon caught up with her and it became inevitable that she'll be married to someone. Mazi Alapa loathed the idea but had to accept realities by inviting her once to his presence.

"You have served me more than any other person have, slave or free born, and I am very grateful. I would have loved to set you free as a mark of my gratitude but that would amount to my cutting my neck to enable me watch and admire my face. I've thought for a very long time of what to do and I've been very unsuccessful. Once, I thought of marrying you but you very well know how our people feel about such things. I have, therefore, decided to ask you to consider yourself free. Several people, slaves and freeborns, have shown desires to marry you. Virtually all my men had whispered the thought to my hearing once or twice. So, feel free and select the one that best suits you. Let me know tomorrow. But before I officially set you free, I'll swear you to our oracle that you'll never run away. I may not be able to bear your absence from the family."

Chinelo was very grateful to her master for setting her partially free. She pledged her continued service to him and promised not to run away. This promise she repeated the following morning in the presence of the oracle and she was sworn to it. That same morning, she became the wife of Mazi Alapa's most handsome retained slaves who had equally been set free but sworn not to run.

After her marriage, Chinelo continued to do most of the household chores of the Alapa family. That was despite repeated calls by Mazi Alapa that she should delegate some of the jobs to other people while she faced her own family of two. She persisted and even took on more responsibilities. Being free, she started making moi moi wraps for the local market, though with Alapa's consent. Alapa, however, refused to have anything to do with her earnings but instead encouraged her and her husband. Soon, "Ada elele's" moi moi became hot cake in the local market and nobody was ever considered to have been to the local market unless he or she bought her moi moi. She soon introduced the fried variety of her baked beans, the more popular "Akara". She literally became the queen of the market. Her fame soon spread to nearby villages. Two years later, it spread into Izombe College, Izombe where the students broke College rules in order to buy akara and moi moi. The intelligent Reverend Father Winterbottom had no alternative than to meet Chinelo and advise that she brought her commodities to sell at the College gate, daily during breaks. That solved the problem for the school and earned Chinelo more money. Everyone was satisfied.

College students, who are never tired of giving people fun names soon changed Chinelo's name to Mama Akara. Chinelo loved the tag even though she hadn't become a mother yet. But she acted like a mother to the poorly fed students and so, was their true mother. She soon knew most of the students by name and all the senior students by their first and nick names.

The name soon became a source of sorrow to her for despite the fact that she had sold akara and moi moi to several generations of College students over twenty five years, she was still not a physical mother. Repeated visits to native doctors were in vain. The last doctor finally advised that he couldn't see anything wrong with her. He, therefore, suggested that the oracle be consulted. It was the oracle that revealed that Idemili, Chinelo's oracle at Inwelle, had sworn never to allow his daughter to have children under the bondage of slavery. That did it. Nobody spoke of children again and Mazi Alapa loved Chinelo so much that he couldn't bear the thought of letting her go. Chinelo, on her part, felt disappointed that she might never have a child of her own. On the other hand she basked on the realisation that her oracle was still protecting her in such a far-off foreign land. She felt reassured that she was not alone. But she pitied her poor husband, who though understood her predicament, would have felt better with a child.

* * * * * *

Ogbuefi Udemba gazed fixedly at the kola that Ogbuefi Ngwu's wife had presented in a wooden plate. A whole fruit of aligator pepper lay passively beside it. The kola was a bright yellow "Ugo" kola irregularly spotted in green.

"Our father," she addressed him to the hearing of all present, 'I have got kola," she said hurriedly and turned to go.

"Our good wife," Ogbuefi Udemba cut her short, "thank you very much for that piece of information and for the kola. We are not blind but we had to wait for you to confirm that the kola belongs to us. We are glad that you have confirmed as well that we are not deaf as well even though we knew this long ago. But our wife," he suddenly called out on the embarrassed shaking woman, "you have not told us what the kola said. We don't eat kola like yam for kola is not food."

"Our father," Ngwu's wife started all over again, "I've always known you to be a good orator. Consequently, I've always avoided you like the Devil bean. Unfortunately, it seems I have fallen into your trap today. I thought all of you know why I invited you all for this small kola. But as this 'ntukalika' has come to deny me in the presence of his relatives, I hasten to repeat that God has done a great thing for me. It is my smallest son, Idigo. They said that he passed to go to College and because he performed so well, the Oyibo people have given him 'Kolachip'."

"Which Idigo?" one of them asked as if that was the first time he was hearing the story. "You don't mean that small rat that is playing with little children outside now," he continued without waiting for his first question to be answered. "I'll never find people trouble any more no matter how small now that I have discovered that too many people are more intelligent than me. So, this little boy can easily sell me?" he asked.

"Fear those little things that don't talk," another advised, "their heads are full of great things to do."

"And where is the child on whose behalf we have gathered?" Ogbuefi Udemba asked just as Idigo's mother was about to settle down and enjoy the pride of being the mother of an intelligent child. "Don't stay there and take all the praises," he spoke to her, "they are't meant for you. None of your kinsmen is intelligent so, call our son for us. If we intelligent people want to discuss, we discuss with other intelligent people. I know how to discuss with you."

The gathering burst out laughing because they've always known that Idigo's mother had a special intimate relationship with Ogbuefi Udemba ever since Ogbuefi Ngwu passed away.

"Tortoise," Idigo's mother labelled her old lover, "only God knows when you'll stop being mischievous."

"When I am sown as people sow yam," Ogbuefi Udemba promptly answered. "How I wish our brother is still alive today to know that a star has arisen in our midst."

"Death is bad," someone added. "It never kills the right person."

They all fell silent when the bright-eyed Idigo was led in by her mother.

"Our son," Ogbuefi Udemba addressed an obviously embarrassed Idigo. "Come and shake me thoroughly. Thank you very much for the lion you killed," he said as he received a reluctant feeble handshake. "Stand by my side because you are the head that was borne in mind while making the cap."

Ogbuefi Udemba looked the crowd from right to left and from left to right to make sure that it was his due honour to break the kola. Mazi Okwundu nodded encouragements to him when his eyes fell on him.

"It seems as if I'm stuck with the kola," Ogbuefi Udemba submitted solemnly to the gathering.

"Do it, it is an entitlement," some voices urged him on as if he needed being urged.

"The flood does not miss the poll," Mazi Okwundu added.

"So, you people have agreed that I should go on. I thank you for that. You have been told why we are gathered here. She did not tell you well because people do not go to school in the villages around us hence, they do not know the importance."

"Where will they obtain the brain from?" Arinze asked sarcastically.

"We know that people from my area do not go to school but they have never asked the Inwelle people for food," Idigo's mother countered. "Worse still, we defeated some people in a land case just two native weeks ago."

"We didn't mention anybody's name," Ogbuefi Udemba added, "so let no one cry. Besides let those who won the land case venture to plant a single yam tuber there and we shall teach them that gun powder catches fire," he said smilingly at Idigo's mother.

"Bless the kola I gave you, our husband," Idigo's mother urged him, "even if Inwelle people cultivate the land, we still know who owns it."

"It is this boy that brought us here," Ogbuefi Udemba finally reminded the crowd as he pointed to Idigo. "He has made us to obtain some of our share of Oyibo things," he continued smilingly to the relief of many who felt that the initial jokes were becoming foul. "Our little son, Idigo, has removed a big shame from our faces. He has firmly placed the name of our family in the good books of Oyibo people even in their land. Everybody Overseas is asking to know more about this young wizard. In houses, markets, streams, taps, offices, churches, everywhere, people are discussing about our son and our family," Ogbuefi Udemba continued his misinformation. "This was because there was one 'sum' which nobody could solve, not even the Oyibo teacher who set it. But Idigo did."

"What shall we call this one?" Mazi Okwundu asked with the thought of everyone overseas speaking of him and his family still dancing about joyously in his mind.

"And when he moves about like a wild bush cat, you'll think he is a dunce," one of Idigo's cousins added.

"But you can always see the intelligent clever eyes which he got from his father," Arinze cut in. "He took totally after his father even in his intelligence except that his father, like every other fellow in our family hadn't an opportunity to show it in books."

"Of all the people who took the examination, he took first position. More still, his "Oyibo" was so good that our teachers here couldn't understand some of the words he used. They had to send some of his work to 'Oyibo land' so that Oyibo people should see real

'Oyibo.'"

"Whom do you call teachers?" Arinze questioned. "I know you don't include that Okeke's son, Johny. He doesn't cook, he doesn't eat and wherever there is a celebration, he'll be fighting over palm wine. He has not spoken to me ever since I denied him the dreg of palm wine our age group obtained during that last funeral at Obodookwe. What we have here are not teachers. How many times do you see Mr. Diapa, the Oyibo teacher that passes here frequently, drinking palm wine?".

"He often buys oranges, pawpaw, guava and eggs any time he passes bye." Idigo's mother added.

"Our father, continue," Arinze urged a smiling Udemba.

"After looking through his work, they decided to send it to the woman King."

"Do you mean that the Queen saw it too?" someone asked in surprise.

"Don't rush me," Ogbuefi Udemba begged. "I am an old man and I forget a lot of things if I'm frequently interrupted."

"You are only old when you want to be mischievous. You are never old when you attack me," Idigo's mother accused to everyone's amusement.

"After reading what Idigo wrote, she decided to give him a 'Kolachip.' It was written there in the letter his headmaster read to us. It said that the Queen, after looking through his performance, had deemed it fit to award him a 'Kolachip' in a college."

"Please, pardon me but what is 'Kolachip'?" someone asked.

"I've seen someone whom I'm better than," Ogbuefi Udemba chipped. "My friend, it means that the queen will pay his school fees in college till our son becomes 'Dokoto', Lawyer or 'Akawo'. We shall put in no penny. They even begged us to allow them to train him and we agreed or didn't we?"

"We did," his relatives readily responded.

"We did well," Ogbuefi Udemba accepted. "That is exactly what his father would have done if he were alive. He loved truth and knowledge," he lied and shook his head to remove the sad memory of Ogbuefi Ngwu's untimely death which had started to settle in his head. 'That is why we have gathered here this evening. Idigo will be leaving

early tomorrow morning to college so we have come to bid him farewell. If you have anything to tell him, do so while we eat our kola ."

Ogbuefi Udemba then proceeded to break the kola."

"Ogbuefi," Mazi Okwundu interrupted him as he broke the kola
into two, "you have not blessed the kola."

Ogbuefi Udemba quickly placed the broken halves together. He
raised the tightly held kola up for all to see.

"Have I broken it?" he smilingly asked.

"No," answered Mazi Okwundu and the rest.

"I was just removing the dry back when one half fell off," he lied
again and raised the kola heaven-wards in prayer.

It was a long prayer which included discussions and lectures.
Finally, he started praying for the individual health of each one
present. Idigo was the last.

"Our son, Idigo," he said. "You shall go and come back in peace."
You'll neither meet a bad man nor a bad spirit on your way. Only
good things will find your way and never a bad thing. As you have
brought us a good name, you'll do more. There, you'll even teach
them instead of their teaching you. It is only the people of 'Oyibo'
that presently know us, but we shall like other people to know that
we have just arrived. Any good thing that presents itself in the town
you are going to, you'll get your share. But if a bad thing like disease
comes, let the owners of the land suffer it alone because it is they that
know how to appease their gods. They don't help us in appeasing ours.
Go, learn and come back. Remember that this is only a beginning.
You shall eventually get there," he said pointing at the far horizon to
indicate overseas. "When your father died, people laughed because
there was nobody to mourn him. So, he was buried without a funeral.
But you have emerged to wipe the tears from our eyes. When you
come back you'll bury your father." Then, raising the kola up once
more because his hand had come down during the marathon speech,
he called on the gods of the land.

"Ogwugwu, Aro, Idemili, Nkpukpa, Ukpaka Otolo, Iyi Ojii, Nkisi
and all the gods of our land, come and have kola. The King that lives
in the skies, the greatest, the King that people know but still full of
mysteries, He that destroys and rebuilds, come and have kola. We
don't know how to approach you without incurring your wrath. So,

we meekly approach you kneeling down because it is only by kneeling down that a young goat sucks milk from the mother. We cannot say much but to ask you to take care of our son, Idigo, who is going out in search of 'Oyibo' knowledge. Do more than we can ask. We shall all live," he finally concluded in a raised voice.

"Ise," they all responded.

"Ogbuefi Okaa Omee - o - o - o," they called one after the other.

"It is not easy. You shall all live," he responded and proceed to break the kola. "If you have anything to tell the small boy, you are free to do so."

"Idigo, our son, I have one very small advice to give you," one of his cousins said with a mouthful of kola." You know you have found favour in the eyes of the Oyibo people. Try not to offend them. Be humble, don't fight or steal."

"If that is what you have to say, better forget about that because he knows that more than you. Besides he isn't that type. If it were my son, Chukwuma, that would be different. Have you ever seen Idigo fighting?" Ogbuefi Udemba asked.

"In addition," the man remained undaunted despite the rudeness, "don't leave the school compound except in company of the other students. Even though the Oyibo people have abolished slavery, people are still kidnapped at random. And anytime you meet an indigene of the place call him your In-law. It is by being everyone's in-law that a lot of people go free in the land you are going to."

"Don't move out alone under any circumstance," Ogbuefi Udemba advised.

"Don't play too much," the last speaker concluded.

Thereafter, many people said many things, some very important, others, mere trash. Idigo collected seven shillings four pence before the gathering dispersed except from Ogbuefi Udemba.

"Remember the witchcraft juju around your waist," he reminded Idigo for want of something to say as he waited for night to come, "never remove it from your waist."

"Yes, sir," Idigo responded.

"You can go and sleep for you must wake early and the journey is long."

* * * * * *

Immediately Reverend John Campbell who escorted him left, Idigo made his bed packed his things neatly and left the hostel, Crowder House, for a stroll around the school compound. He walked about aimlessly but avoided the neatly mown grass verges and flower beds. He was impressed by what he saw and was still enjoying himself when the bell rang for lunch. It was a welcomed information for, for two days running, he had not tasted an oil meal.

Idigo ran back to his hostel and quietly retrieved his cutlery from his locker. He ultimately joined the thronging crowd for the Dining Hall where he was taught the right use of the cutlery by a form two boy. He couldn't eat much but was forced to leave his unfinished meal when it was time to leave.

Back in the hostel, he was too tired and had barely laid this head on the pillow when he made off. He was still sleeping when the others left for one thing or the other, though, it was time for games. He was still sleeping when it was "games over".

"Who is around," a small boy occupying a bed two beds away from Idigo's suddenly called out.

All the form one students around ran to answer him. Idigo, who had just woken could barely raise his legs off the grass mattress on his six-spring bed. He heard the call quite alright but never knew it was intended for him. After all, the boy could see him very well, if he had wanted him, he would have made that clear, Idigo, indeliberately ignored the call.

"My God," exclaimed the boy who was popularly referred to as Iron Monger. "Mr. Frog, so you didn't hear me?" Iron Monger asked pointing in Idigo's direction.

Idigo saw him quite alright but thought Iron Monger was referring to someone beyond him. He was surprised to find nobody behind him.

"So, this small toad," he said in feigned anger and surprise. "So, you didn't hear me? Are you deaf?"

"I'm sorry," Idigo politely apologised. "I didn't know you were referring to me."

"Even when I called you Mr. Frog?" Iron Monger pressed on.

"My nickname is not Mr. Frog. My Mother calls me Idigomgom but my uncles and cousins call me Engineer Nwa Ogalanya." My real name is Idigo U. 'U' is for Umunna," Idigo took the pains to explain.

"There is nothing I can't see in this school," complained Iron Monger. "A toad, not even a toad, a mere tad-pole, telling me, the honourable Iron Monger, who has swallowed enough stone from the school rice to build a house with and who has eaten enough bean weevils to qualify for an award, to call him Idi . . ., Idi . . . What? and Engineer Nwa Ogalanya. An abomination has happened for which you must be punished to appease the gods of this hostel."

Other Crowderians burst out laughing at the drama. It was then that it occurred to Idigo that the Society he then found himself was not as simple as the lawns and flower beds he saw. It became obvious to him that he had over estimated his friendship with his tormentors and was bound to pay dearly for his careless talks.

"King Idigomgom alias Engineer Nwa Ogalanya," Iron Monger called, "your lordship, kindly have the humility of coming down from your gold throne in an ivory tower built in the wind and honour the floor of my bed side with your knees."

Idigo promptly obeyed.

"Hands up, eyes close, mouth open," Iron monger commanded.

Idigo followed each command with immediate action. He felt very embarrassed and couldn't find his voice to beg for mercy.

He remained in that humble position until everybody had left the dark hostel. He was still kneeling though with his eyes open and mouth closed when the House Prefect, Double Tragedy, entered. He failed to notice Idigo at the perfectly dark corner where he was kneeling down. His knees were aching terribly and any slight movement sent sharp pains racing through his small frame. He thought fast of a way to liberty.

"Senior, Please?" he politely called questioningly.

"Who is that?" Tragedy responded rudely.

"Senior, it is me Master Idigo 'U'," Idigo answered fast. "A senior from Mogo House was here looking for you," Idigo lied.

"What is his name?" the unsuspecting prefect asked.

"He refused to give his name but preferred to repeat later this night," Idigo continued.

"That is fine. But what are you doing there in the dark corner beside the bed of a senior student?" the prefect asked suspiciously.

"Senior, I am under punishment."

"By whom?"

"By Senior Iron Monger."

"What was your crime?"

"Senior, he complained that I didn't respond to his call fast enough."

"Since when?" the prefect continued his seemingly unnecessary querry.

"Senior, since about half past five this evening," Idigo continued to answer at about seven o'clock.

The prefect was visibly annoyed but there was no way Idigo would have known. The prefect had always warned his hostel members to avoid terrorising junior students more so, new students, But it seemed Iron Monger didn't hear and should be terrorised himself when he came back.

"Don't disobey your seniors," Double Tragedy advised in a voice which failed to betray his annoyance, "answer their calls promptly. You have come here, not for book studies alone but to purify and discipline your mind also. The combination of academics and self-discipline makes a fully total man. Always remember this. It will help you throughout life to help build a civilised society free from fear and want. You can go."

Idigo was already up before the prefect could finish his lecture on life. He fell on his first attempt to stand and had to sit briefly on Iron Monger's bed before he finally rose. He thanked the prefect profusely before leaving the hostel. He swore never to be caught for punishment again little knowing that the rat never gets caught in a trap under sober conditions.

* * * * * *

Senior Toochi, a form four student of Ogoazi House was so sure of where his pair of new Latin textbooks were that he didn't bother to look. Immediately he came by his window, he put his right hand through it to the top of his locker. His hand never made any contact with any book. He swept his hand both left and right, forwards and backwards over the top of the locker but with little success. He took three stops backwards.

"One, two, three, four," he counted the windows from his left. "One, two, three, four, five, six, seven," he counted the rest from his right. Between these two sets of windows was his window.

He went back to the window from where he took the steps. A repeat search for the books was abortive. He was forced against his wish to go round the hostel block into the hostel. It was a wasted exercise as none of the books could be found anywhere. Convinced that one of his close friends or disciplined "toads" had done him the favour of taking up his books to the prep-room, he hastened to the prep area. He was very optimistic when he entered the room. He expected someone to beacon him to his books. Unfortunately, no such welcome awaited him. He went round the prep room enquiring from friends, 'toads", class and Hostel mates but drew a blind end. Toochi had no other alternative than to consult his house prefect, Sokija.

"Let it not be true that western things have started happening in the East," Sokija announced to an amazed group of expectant students. "Senior Tojaa have just reported the loss or misplacement of two of his latin textbooks. I wouldn't believe that they were stolen because the likes have never happened in our house and the entire school before. Hence, if you have any idea as to where these books are to be found, feel at ease to inform him or me. If, however, you are in possession of these books, save yourself the pains of being found out by placing them where they can easily be found. You have been advised."

By the following Friday morning, the books were still at large. Consequently, a search was organised by the House Prefect and his deputy in Ogoazi House. The search, which was organised with the permission of the House Master, went on fine until they got to the fifteenth bed.

"Ugoka O., open your box," the prefect ordered.

Senior Ugoka made an effort to open his box, took back his hands. He went to his locker, came back, fumbled under his pillow and did one odd thing or the other. He shook visibly to the surprise and suspicion of others present.

"Open your box," the excited prefect repeated in jubilation that the culprit had most probably been discovered.

Senior Ugoka O. made a desperate attempt to open his box and dare the consequences but his courage failed him. He just sat down on his bed covering his face in his hands.

The more daring deputy House Prefect moved with lightning speed and pushed the box open.

A stampede ensued as each member of the small search party made for the exit at the shortest possible time.

* * * * * *

Idigo was enjoying the Mathematics lessons very well when the school bell started ringing. There wasn't anything odd about the school bell ringing at the time it did except that it was ringing continuously at a uniform rate which meant that there is an emergency condition. According to school rule which Idigo then knew at his finger tips, such a ringing pattern signified that something serious had occurred requiring the immediate attention of the entire student body.

Immediately the fat Mathematics Master left the classroom, Idigo quickly put back his books, pen and ruler into his desk locker and ran with the other students to the Assembly Hall, which was by then packed full of people. Idigo slowly but steadily edged himself to the middle seats of the Assembly Hall where a friend of his created a sitting space for him on the hard long bench. They were bursting with enthusiasm to hear from the Principal what sort of event could necessitate an emergency assembly. It was a novelty for Idigo, his mates and the two classes below him because for the past three years he was in the school, he had never had such an assembly before.

The students were still arguing on why the state of emergency when the burly-looking Principal arrived. He literally flowed into the Assembly Hall and went up the platform. A look at his face convinced even the greatest optimist that the end of the world was at hand. He promptly motioned on the standing students to sit down.

"It is with a sad heart, heavy with grief and disappointment that I received the news this morning that some of my sudents have come down to such mean levels of practicing witchcraft in my school," Mr. Winterbottom announced to the perplexed body. "All of you are children of God and you pray to Him everyday for protection and provisions. You read His Holy Words daily and promise in your prayers to keep his commandments. One of these is that you should serve no other god than Him. What then do you do with those pieces of dry leaves, dry meat, feather, ash and all other types of rubbish tied in dirty pieces of leather? What do you do with your so-called charms?" he asked an ice-cold assembly.

Idigo's testicles disappeared into his turning stomach. He had never prayed to the charm in his box and had never thought of it as a substitute to God. All that he knew was that it protected him from witchcraft and other evil forces. He never thought it bad or sinful to possess charms. He had never even confessed its possession in his prayers because it served a good purpose and therefore, must come from God. An evil charm cannot drive away an evil spirit; a good charm cannot come from the devil. The Principal had said that they were rubbish but when has it become a crime for someone to carry some rubbish in one's box? However, these were not his immediate headache. His most pressing problem was that he had one rubbish in his box and no one would believe it was protective not offensive. He then started blaming himself for not wearing it around his waist as was recommended. But how could he bathe with such a dirty string around his waist in an open school bathing room? He looked up for inspiration but none was forthcoming. He was still battling with his thoughts when all the Crowder House inmates ware called out for a search. He followed the others passively to the assembly point in front of their house. The Principal waited outside with the other House Masters, Senior, Labour and Dining Hall Prefects while the Crowder House inmates were called in one after the other. The rest of the students were locked up in the Assembly Hall. Idigo seemed at a loss on what to do when he was beaconed into the hostel. He walked assuredly to the hostel and as he passed the hostel door, he saw a bucket half full with charms of different sizes, shapes, colours and most probably, functions and potency. He smiled.

"At least," he thought, "I'm not alone."

Unfortunately, that courage was brief for, on seeing the imposing figure of the House Master beside his bed, he developed cold feet.

"Umunna I, open you box for inspection," he demanded.

"Yes, Sir," he responded passively with his mind very far away from the event at hand.

Idigo surveyed the hostel block fast and immediately made up his mind on what to do.

The hostel door was the only entrance and exit left open for the search purpose. A window at the far end of the hostel acted, in consonance with the door for ventilation.

"No, your locker first," the master corrected himself.

Idigo obeyed and cautiously opened his locker. Nothing was found therein.

"Your box then," the Master directed.

Idigo obliged, The House Prefect and his deputy were directly behind him and blocked his orthodox route of escape. The tired House Master was sitting beside the prefects on the bed of Idigo's neighbour. Idigo summed up the situation quickly as he slowly opened his box. That was the zero hour. Idigo acted fast.

Idigo picked up the piece of paper covering his scanty collection of oversized second-hand dresses. He dumped it on the bed near the House Master. That distracted some attention as the House Master turned the paper up and down suspiciously. That gave Idigo the little extra time he needed. By the time the Master and the Prefects looked up, Idigo had moved like lightning past his bed and was successfully scaling that of his neighbour on the other side of his bed. By the time the three inspectors could suppress the natural urge to laugh at what they were seeing, Idigo was busy competing with fresh air for access for use of the second source of ventilation, the open window.

"He is running, catch am!" the House prefect shouted.

The deputy and the House Master each shouted for help. Their clarion call attracted the whole people outside including the Principal. All converged eagerly at the only official exit waiting for the kill. Their high hopes were dashed when an agile figure in white pair of shorts and shirts emerged like lightning from the off-hand window clutching something tightly in his left hand. All attempts to halt his rapid movement with shouts proved in vain and the race had began.

Idigo ran like an antelope in an uncharted course which would have led to the school gate. It would have, except that the students from the Assembly Hall joined the rat race thereby blocking his path to the then visible school gate.

Though not prepared for such unforseen impediments, Idigo acted by reflex; he turned right into a small gully developing in front of Doomaby House. The small gully emptied him into the road.

As his pursuers made the road, he instinctively headed for the forested big gully which formed a mesh work of falling rough terrain a few meters off the School compound.

Once out of sight, he summoned all his reserve energy, bent slightly backwards and hauled what he was holding far into the bush of the gully. He then heaved a very big sigh of relief, found a stone and rested briefly before his pursuers arrived and took him captive. They forced open his hand and found not even a trace that he once held something with that hand.

* * * * * *

Idigo mowed the vast grass lawn adjacent the school library with the zeal of one very much convinced of his crimes. That was the third and maybe, the final day of a series of punishments for a series of crimes announced by the school's Senior Prefect. The worst of these crimes wasn't the possession of charm anyway. To Idigo's satisfaction, they accepted that what he threw away was a love letter he received from a girls' school, a newby established sister school. Though it was a serious crime for discplined students to write and receive love letters, Idigo preferred the shame and punishment due for such receipt to the embarrassment and expulsion or suspension for possession of charms. Consequently, he did his grass cutting, which was a follow-up to six strokes of the cane, with comparative gladness.

However, by the evening of that third day, his back and waist ached seriously. He persisted until the bell for dinner went by 6.30 p.m.

"Today na Rice-Bean Jollof, RBJ," he muttered to his langalanga (cutlass), "Today na party day."

The sound of the 6.30 p.m. bell was a welcome relief to Idigo whose entrails were already on the verge of being torn to shreds by mere hunger. He rose from his bent position with much pain from virtually all his joints and looked momentarily at the remains of work to be done. It wasn't much but work was still work; it is never embraced with open arms. Not demoralised by the friendly bell, Idigo threw the cutlass in a spinning motion upwards. He watched it go up and caught it by its handle on its descent, raised it up and pointed it in the direction of the Dining Hall. He instantly followed the direction of his cutlass.

The thought of the evening meal still danced about his sharp brain as he passed the Principal's office on his way to the Dining Hall. From this Office, he could see the swarm of students who climbed over each other to buy one thing or the other from the women traders. Idigo needed no more information. The meal was RBJ, the popular name for Rice and Beans Jollof. He weighed the hunger in his stomach and quickly concluded that it wasn't the type a complex mixture of rice and beans, liberally mixed with an ample amount of stones and bean weevils, could satisfy. He felt his right short pocket and the two pennies there asked him to change direction. He obeyed and ultimately found his way to the School gate. Not being gifted with struggling for things, he greeted mama Elele as he arrived and stayed aside for the crowd to thin out. Chinelo saw him where he was standing, tied four big wraps of 'elele' and put them aside under her basket.

Idigo was still standing away from the ever increasing crowd when Chinelo announced that "elele" was finished. He was dismayed and sighs of disappointment that sounded from different parts of the turbulent crowd showed he wasn't alone in his disappointment.

"You mean all the "elele" are finished?" Idigo asked in disbelief.

"Idigo, my son," Chinelo avoided the question, "so you are still doing punishment for that small race of last Friday."

"Na waa!" Idigo answered absentmindedly as the last boy left for the hostel. "But don't you have even a wrap left?" he persisted.

Chinelo opened her mouth to answer and a big yawn of tiredness escaped her mouth.

"These children," she exclaimed, "they are becoming rougher with each passing year. Let Idemili forbid evil," she swore as she handed him the four big wraps of "elele" she had reserved for him under the basket.

Idigo wasn.t surprised that she reserved some for him. In fact, he would have been surprised if she didn't reserve some for him. It had become a routine for Chinelo was very fond of that quiet intelligent boy with an over sized head and bulging bright eyes. He reminded her of someone she knew very intimately. Who that someone was she wouldn't know.

"Thank you ma," Idigo greeted as he handed her half a penny for the worth of the parcel. He had half-turned to go when he decided to exploit his intimacy with her. "But I heard you swear by Idemili now? It seems everyone uses this name nowadays, even those that do not know what it stands for."

"Idemili?" Chinelo asked defiantly as she packed her load.

"Don't call it with the casuality of someone eating tapioca," Idigo objected. "It is a very powerful god."

"Are you telling me the Idemili you know, the Idemili you were told or the one you read from your Oyibo books?" She smilingly enquired.

"The Idemili I know," the soft-spoken boy answered in triumph.

"I know her more than you," she happily informed him. "Your books don't tell you everything. The Oyibos say the ones they were told and no more. I am a true born daughter of Idemili," she proudly announced.

Idigo watched the smiling lady as she busied herself packing her things.

"Nothing can bring a true child of Idemili all this far except education. No true daughter of Inwelle should be married so far away from home. No free daughter of Idemili should be married to these people who devour the royal python," he thought as Chinelo smile victoriously.

Idigo helped her place her load on her head and instantly hurried to the Dining Hall not very sure to meet his meals. He turned once to know whether Chinelo had gone far and saw a brief outline of her disappearing into dusk.

"Many people claim what they are not," he muttered to himself. "What is that thing they are called?" he asked himself as he went. "Ehmm, Impostor." A classmate of his agreed as they passed each other. "He claims to be highly religious but loves seizing people's meals daily."

Idigo looked up to see the Dining Hall prefect following the boy that serves him to his hostel. The boy was carrying a big plate of food.

"Yes, an impostor," Idigo readily agreed even though the Prefect was not the impostor he initially meant.

* * * * * *

"Mama a nata, o - Yo - Yoo," the first voice announced as its owner sighted the slim old woman coming back late from the market.

Before this scout could repeat that broadcast, a mixture of fine and hoax children's voices have taken the cue. Each announced excitedly and independently, the arrival of the much awaited grandmother. The children drowned the neighbourhood with their song and wild shouts. None of the numerous children stood still while he or she sang. On the contrary, each was in top speed as each tried desperately to get to Idigo's mother first.

The old frail woman, with a basket of virtually everything in the market, saw the reception from the army of children as they raced towards her. It was a routine practice she had grown up to meet. The older children were growing too powerful for her but she had no way of letting them know that her moon was waning. She brazed herself for the assault of the first arrivals because it is by use of sensible tactics that an elder runs away from a mad cow. She placed one foot behind, held her basket with one hand and used the other hand to break the force of the young sprinters.

"My children," Idigo's mother called the teeming crowd amidst shouts of "Mama, welcome, Mama welcome," "I hope you looked after the house," she said as she placed the basket on top the head of the biggest boy. She inspected the children closely for wounds and bruises which were not uncommon among village children. Satisfied that no serious fight had erupted among the children in her absence, she carried the youngest of the children and led the way back to her sun-baked mud house which have seen a lot of sun and rain.

Idigo heard the shouts of the children from his room. He was very grateful to the children for acting as very efficient look-out scouts who always informed him of the arrival of his mother. He swiftly swung his pair of dust-free feet off the cheap blanket covering a much dishevelled gross-filled mattress. He dropped the novel he was reading and hid it under his small but clean bare pillow. With his feet, he quickly found his pair of bathroom slippers, clad his feet with them and hurriedly left the room for the backyard.

When Idigo's mother entered the house with her entourage, she saw Idigo coming out from his pet vegetable farm. Idigo greeted her from that point and she was glad that Idigo, the good child, had taken her advice, that constant reading causes nervous breakdown, very seriously.

"How was the market?" he inquired as he came nearer.

"Nothing seems to sell nowadays but I managed to sell the two bundles of bitter-leaf I took along as well as the cocoyam," she answered as she unloaded her purchases. "But I was unlucky with the bitters I took along. The entire market was full of them," she complained.

"Edible things are never bad trade commodities. It will never be a waste. They at the worst, end up in the owner's stomach," Idigo consoled. "Better still, when they cannot be easily sold and the owner is ill-disposed to consume them, they can be preserved for later periods of scarcity."

"I have not time to dry bitters. I have more important things to do. My hands are full with much work to be done in the farm. I was even so annoyed that I tactfully left it under my market seat."

"But mama, during the dry season these bitters are scarce commodities, why not prepare for the rainy day," he asked.

"For bitters?" she asked contemptuously. "Oh well, I can't go back to the market for them, besides, I'm not wiser than the other women who did the same."

Idigo's mind's eye flew immediately to the market scene with unsold oranges, bananas, spinach, water leaf, pumpkin, mangoes and other fruits and vegetables littering an otherwise beautiful scenery to the happiness and choruses of houseflies and bees. He loathed the apparent insensitivity of the people to the abundant wastage of periodic fruits and vegetables. He found it difficult to accredit such indifference to short-sightedness because the people were quite aware that the period of scarcity was sure to follow. It wasn't laziness because they worked hard for some of these fruits and vegetables and hoped to do so again, come the next planting season.

"This is sheer lunacy, short-lived but recurrent lunacy," he found himself saying as he walked towards his room where he became engulfed in thought as to the best way of preserving most of the farm produce. He was still absorbed in thought when he overheard his name mentioned outside.

* * * * * *

Idigo overheard the message and had no doubt that a parcel was due for him. He momentarily changed his thought from the abundant waste to which his people are prone and concentrated on what the parcel contained. He was still involved in this unnecessary hobby when the messenger breezed in, dropped the parcel with an accompanying message and rushed out with the speed with which he entered. He was rushing so as not to get an unfair share of the thing grandmother bought them.

Idigo's hand immediately set to work to unwrap the not too bulky parcel neatly covered over with plantain leaf. He had always begged his mother to forget about buying him such petty edible things from the market. He felt he was a grown-up and that such things should be reserved for children only. In addition, hard-earned cash should be used a bit more prudently on more important things. But his mother would not believe he was a grown up despite the fact that he had just finished his secondary education, having taken his Cambridge examination.

His disapproval didn't stop him from probing into the inner contents of the parcel as he removed one plantain leaf after another. Finally, his probe landed him on two oily wraps and three balls of akara.

"I would have known better," Idigo thought as he threw some dry coats of the fried akara balls into his mouth. He eyed the partly burnt oily plantain leaves very suspiciously. He very much suspected it could be "elele" wraps but it could possibly be its senior brother,

"Ikpa-oka" which is made from maize grains. This was more common at that period of abundant maize than the sweeter "elele". In addition, it was also more difficult to chew. Idigo never loved it but the olders said it was the best food to be thought of.

Idigo pressed one of the oily wraps and it felt soft. "Ikpa-oka" wouldn't be as soft as that but who knows. It wasn't impossible that the maker had over-added water to the mixture. He proceeded to unwrap one of the wraps. He was half way when he noticed that the highly appetising aroma coming off his hands were better than that of baked corn meal. But he proceeded with his enquiry. He had started seeing part of the oil-yellow baked beans contoured beautifully with rings of onions and spiced with partly ground red pepper. A small rebellious quantity of the cake made a desperate attempt to resist being eaten. Idigo expertly intercepted it with his left hand between his right hand, holding the "elele" wrap, and the mud floor. He smiled at his agility and was glad that the culprit was the child of a very sweet baked beans cake. He put out his head to the door and after repeated trials, one of the noisy children surrounding his mother managed to get his thanks through.

Idigo went back to his room and the cakes and masterfully but slowly ate up the tiny specks of "elele" surrounding the main mountain.

"These cakes can't be eaten alone," he mused to himself. "Half cup of garri, a mixture of salt and sugar are needed to honour it," he concluded. "Ifeomah," he called out without success. "Ifeomah," he repeated a little louder.

"Ify, Ify Ify," a couple of children repeated outside before the message got to the person intended.

Ifeomah, Idigo's niece ran towards his room to answer the call.

"Ifeomah, remember that we are on very good terms," one of the children reminded her.

"Go away," another protested, "you've forgotten that she is my sister," Ify's junior sister reminded the others.

"I gave you some star-apple the other day," yet another refreshed her memory.

"I am coming," was all Ifeomah could say as she ran on expecting some good.

But by the time she got to the door, the boy who originally sent the parcel to Idigo had effectively blocked the door.

"Idigo, I was the one who brought you the parcel. Mama said that I should take away the refuse to the goat house after you have eaten," he lied.

"Alright, I'll call you after," Idigo promised.

The disappointed but still optimistic boy left the door for Ifeomah to enter.

"Brother, they said you called me."

"Go and find out if we still have garri in that salt bag," Idigo directed her much to her disappointment.

"I brought some this afternoon and as you are the only one that eats it in the whole house, it should still be there."

"Then get me about half a cup," he told her. "Bring salt also," he added as she ran off for the garri expecting some reward thereafter.

"What did he ask for?" his mother asked Ifeomah as she sped past.

"Garri and salt."

"What is he going to do with garri this late evening?"

"He wants to eat the cakes with it."

"I-D," the mother called pettingly, "what do you say you want to do with garri?"

"Mama, to eat these cakes," came the humble answer.

"Chei!" exclaimed the mother. "What type of college did you attend?" She querried.

Idigo smiled at the surprised signs on her mother's face.

"Mama, what is so odd about it?" He asked innocently.

"It is very demeaning. People have to overgrow things. Your type of college surprises me. Frequently, I wonder whether the one you attended was the same as that the people of Guru do. I forced you to stop eating pounded cassava against your wish. That was only last two holidays but I know that others stop immediately they enter college. Even now, I know you eat it outside this house thereby rubbing charcoal on my face. There is no type of food you don't eat even though others restrict themselves to garri, rice and yam. You are a big disgrace."

"But mama, what is wrong in what people eat provided it doesn't make them feel bad or less intelligent?"

"There are certain things that people who have learnt the Oyibo book shouldn't do. How many times do your teachers eat pounded cassava, drink palm wine or Kaikai? A trained person should eat fruits, drink Oyibo drinks if he has money. The only Oyibo food I wouldn't subscribe to is eggs. It makes people steal and produces too much foul gas in the stomach. Soaked garri is the last thing a trained college boy should take. People say it spoils the eye."

"Mama, doctor," Idigo laughed. "Who told you garri spoils the eye?"

"You argue too much. That is the problem with you learned people. Garri is not good for your eyes. Whether you believe it or not, it is still true."

"I've always believed it," Idigo joked, "but you forced it on me at home despite the fact that I preferred cassava. If it spoils my eye, you are then responsible."

"I recommended garri soaked in hot water, not cold. The hot water kills off all the bad things that cause trouble in garri," she lectured masterfully to Idigo's appreciation.

"Like hot water kills the ones that cause trouble in pounded cassava yet you preferred garri," Idigo chipped in.

"I'm too tired for your arguments today. Don't use me to practice 'lawyer'. The eyes belong to you. Spoil them with garri. If the ones at home won't be sufficient, let me order for a bag for you. It's all my fault. If I didn't buy the garri, you wouldn't have misused it. Go on, koll yourself with it. There are glasses in the market but not for blind men."

"Mama, you may be correct," Idigo appeased her enraged mother. "But I've been drinking garri from my first day in the college to the last. It means that either soaked garri doesn't disturb sight or if it does, it hasn't affected mine. And as it hasn't spoilt my eye up till now, it will never do so in future," Idigo boasted.

"Drink garri in College?" his initially disinterested mother suddenly asked.

"Yes. It is a popular practice," Idigo infomed.

"Who gives it to you?"

"Sometimes, the school gives it when they are not able to prepare the normal food on the time-table. Sometimes, we buy it ourselves.

"And drink it alone?" she continued in surprise.

"Sometimes. But frequently, the school serves it with tinned fish or beans. Personally, most students take it with groundnuts, coconuts, fried bread fruit, palm kernels, akara and "elele.""

"You people should better tell us that it is not books that you go to study in the colleges. But waste all your time eating all the types of food that we eat at home. Then tell me what you go to learn in school?"

"Books and how to better the life of our people."

"By eating akara and 'elele'?" Idigo's mother asked sarcastically.

Idigo didn't feel like continuing the argument because he was sure they weren't seeing things from the same angle. And any attempt to enlighten his mother would only infuriate her. He let things slip bye. His mother took it for capitulation and fired on to victory.

"And who taught the bush people of Izombe to make akara and 'elele'?" she demanded. "Lies should have limits. We heard that learned people like lawyers tell a lot of lies and I was doubting. But now, I believe. While telling a lie some other time, find better ones," she advised.

Idigo felt his credibility was seriously in doubt and didn't want to leave it that way. He loathed a lot of things in life and that included the thought of being thought of as a liar.

"We eat akara and 'elele' in school," Idigo maintained.

"The people of Izombe wouldn't know how to make them, that is all I know. It is only an art practised by the people around Guru. Even the people down the big river don't know it. The coconut people, for sure, are ignorant of it," she argued.

"But we eat it at Izombe," Idigo held on stubbornly not sure what to say.

"Who makes them then, ghosts?"

It was then that Idigo thought of the people that made akara and 'elele' for them. His thought centred on Mama 'elele' and he cursed himself for forgetting that good woman so much in a hurry. She had been very fond of him in school and by his final year in school they were like mother and son. Yet, Idigo never knew for sure from where mama 'elele' came. She was married to an Izombe man and was supposed to be from Izombe. But he wasn't very sure she comes from Izombe because her intonation was very different.

* * * * * *

Senior Idigo felt as free as air as he came down the short steps of the Examination Hall, the school's Assembly Hall. He heard the other candidates discussing the last paper excitedly and felt slightly jealous that nobody seemed to find the paper difficult. Not that he, himself, found it so but whenever a paper was difficult he felt more at ease because, it was only then that he seemed more sure to prove his excellence. He was never in the habit of discussing past papers with anybody so, he walked quietly away towards his hostel. He was more quiet than usual as he passed some form four boys sitting down on one of the steps on the grass lawns leading to the hostel area. He was so pre-occupied in his mind that he failed to hear the friendly greetings of the three junior students.

"Latin has passed the 'mensa' stage," one of them commented.

"Senior Idigo seems to have seen too much fire from the Latin paper," another readily agreed.

"In this workd?" the third asked. "Impossible. His head is full of brains. One half of his grey matter is made of Latin."

"You don't know what you are saying. Ask his mates who owns the Latin class if not all the other subjects." A fourth student supported. "He may be just tired of the entire examination exercise."

"Many of them haven't seen sleep for the past two weeks since the examination started," the second speaker concurred so as to be in line.

"Maybe, he may be feeling sad about leaving school," the first speaker suggested. "Leaving friends isn't the best passing-out gift."

"Ah!" exclaimed the last speaker. "Many of them will be leaving tomorrow or next after the house feasts and send-off parties tonight."

"So, I've become the most senior student of this school from today. And exactly three hundred and sixty five days today, I'll be leaving too," announced the third boy.

They all shook hands with each other at their accomplishments which included being in form four and being tentative prefects. They thereafter, disbanded to their various hostels to supervise the preparations for the feasts and house parties.

Idigo, ignorant of the analyses and self-conceit of the four prefect-designates, continued his slow and steady motion with all the problems the prefects enumerated, bugging his life. By the time he got to the hostel, his primary concern was to see Mama "elele" as fast as possible. For more than a week, he hadn't the opportunity to do so. But throughout the examination, the thought of her never ceased crossing his congested mind. He couldn't resist the urge any further by the time he made the corridor of his hostel.

He beaconed the boy that helped him, handed him his examination materials and directly retraced his footsteps to the front of the Principal's Office. Here, he turned left along the dusty untarred road to the school gate.

Idigo tagged along behind two students whose destination was very obvious by the way they smiled. He kept behind them until they came before Mama Elele.

"Mama Elele, how much do you sell cakes today?" one of the boys inquired.

"The price is still the same," she politely answered.

"That is five for half penny," Idigo mischievously added with a modified voice from behind the students.

"Idemili forbid evil," she swore. "Even if you had planted the beans for me and given me oil free-of-charge, what of the salt, pepper and onions?"

"Then sell for us at four and half," Idigo pleaded.

"The last price is three for half a penny. No more, no less," she announced with all finality.

"Mama Elele, we used to buy the cakes six," Idigo lowered the price when he discovered that Mama Elele wasn't swallowing the bait.

"Maybe you steal the extra three or you used juju on me. Bye the way, let me see the masquerade who buys cakes at ten for mere laughter," she said as she pushed the two boys aside to have a better view. "No wonder who'll be doing this type of thing."

"Pack the entire basket of cakes for the boys. They've been patronising you for how long now, why not patronise them once,"

Idigo joked.

"Carry me and give them as well," she offered.

"If you mean it, I'll carry you and take you home myself," Idigo opted.

"Thief, what will you do with somebody's wife?" she asked.

"I'll give her husband back his money and take her back to a civilised world where the beautiful woman belong," Idigo jokingly answered.

"What will your so-called civilized world do with an old woman?" she pursued.

"The beautiful lady would be making her sweet cakes for people like her, civilised people," Idigo answered as if he taped the conversation in his brain.

"And which place is more civilised that Izombe with a college, a church and a dispenser?" she asked her amused teacher.

"And that is not a question one would expect from a true daughter of Idemili. I have warned you before against the frequent use of Idemili's name." Idigo continued in feigned anger. "Idemili will one day deal with you for using its name very vainly," he informed the reclusive Mama Elele.

She raised up her head, smiled as she looked intently on Idigo for some seconds. Idigo felt embarrassed more so when the small tears had suddenly appeared on Mama Elele's eyes indicative of embarrassment. The weary smile was mirthless and didn't convince Idigo that he hadn't committed a serious error of judgement. They looked at each other for quite an eternity. But Mama Elele wasn't really seeing Idigo. What she saw on Idigo's face were people much older than Idigo, people old enough to be Idigo's fathers and grandfathers.

"You've spoken so much of Idemili and defended it so much as if you know much," she accused him mildly. "What towns do you know in Idemili?" She eventually asked to break his embarrassment.

"All," Idigo answered, "Inwelle, Guru," Idigo counted, "in fact, all."

"Whom do you know in Guru?" she asked.

"Our In-laws," Idigo promptly answered.

"Are they marrying from your people or your people are marrying their daughter?"

"They married from our place," Idigo found himself answering.

"Who did they marry?" Mama Elele pressured.

"One of my aunts but I don't know her well because she died long before I was born."

"And what is the name of your village?"

"Inwelle, the land where people thicken their soup with fresh fish."

Mama Elele was glad that Idigo had overcome his embarrassment but still unsuspicious.

"Inwelle . . . . Inwelle . . . . . Inwelle," she pretended to recount where she heard that name before. "Whom do you know there?" She asked even though she was aware it was a stupid question.

"Whom do you know yourself?"He asked back.

"Do you know Mazi Okwundu?" She asked cautiously.

"That is my uncle," Idigo answered promptly. "How do you know him?" He asked in surprise.

"And Ogbuefi Udemba?" She continued ignoring his question.

"Look at this, woman; He is my senior uncle."

"What of Ogbuefi Ngwu?" She persisted.

"This discussion has passed a joke? Who do you say you are, woman?" Idigo asked back.

"The daughter of Idemili. Answer my question," she begged.

"He is my father."

"And Arinze Egwuonwu and others," she asked quickly to cover her sadness which was becoming obvious on her face.

"They are fine," he answered even though a lot of people have died among the others.

"You'll be going tomorrow?" She finally asked.

"No, next tomorrow," he corrected.

"Anytime you go, greet them all for me," she demanded.

"But who do I say greeted?"

"Just tell them that a daughter of Idemili greeted."

Idigo was puzzled by the revelation as much as Chinelo was. He tried desperately for more information but met a very strong smiling walled fence. On her part, Chinelo resisted a strong urge to clasp Idigo on her chest and weep. This would have led to a formal introduction which was against her oath not to contact home or plan an escape. "Don't forget to inform them," she reminded him as she handed him four cakes without charge. Idigo thanked her but regretted missing her.

"We may see again if you greet them," she reminded him. "Don't forget."

Idigo promised not to, bade her farewell and made his way to the hostel. He was so sure that he'll forget. He thought of what to do. At last, he picked a fresh branch of Tridax plant on the road and kept it in his box to help him remember.

Chinelo wept softly all the way home. She had packed immediately after Idigo left, giving away her remaining cakes to the students present. They suspected that something had gone wrong but none bothered less. All the way home, Chinelo mourned.

"So, I've been living with my brother all this while and never knew?" She asked herself intermittently. "But thank God, I've always treated him as a brother and son. Blood is thicker than water. Blood doesn't lie. All the time, we smelt our common blood. Thanks be to God," she murmured home.

Her husband didn't miss the sad expression but was duly informed that market was bad. Though he wasn't sold to the idea, it kept him at bay.

*   *   *   *   *   *

Idigo thought of what became of the piece of herb he placed in his box. Then he remembered seeing it a day after this meeting in his box. He thought it was brought in with the cloths he spread on the mown lawns to dry. He remembered throwing it away through the window with his left hand quite ignorant of the message it was supposed to deliver.

"Idigo, are you still there?" Idigo's mother asked when he didn't speak for a long time. His positive response and that of the children clustering around his door post arrived simultaneously to the inclined and suspicious ears of his mother.

"Only God knows what you are doing silently there in the dark," the mother added.

"Mama, I've just remembered something," Idigo solemnly announced. By the tone of his voice, his mother knew that whatever it was that Idigo remembered was of immense importance to him. "Mama Elele is from either Guru or Inwelle," he added after a delayed thought.

"Who is mama Elele?" his surprised mother asked having either forgotten what they were discussing or unable to correlate the fact that any woman who makes bean cakes automatically becomes the mother of bean cakes. "The woman that makes bean cakes for us at Izombe," Idigo soberly answered. Idigo's mother started laughing.

"So, they have infected you with the sickness prevalent among intelligent and learned people?" she mockingly asked. "But it took you so long to formulate this lie. My son but what a poor liar you are? How did you know she is from Guru or Inwelle?" she finally asked in triumph.

"She told me so or rather, she told me she is a daughter of Idemili," Idigo said undoubtedly.

"And who is her father," she asked.

"I don't know her father's name or even hers. We call her only Mama Elele. She is married to an Izombe man."

"Enough of those lies," his mother warned, "and enough of this silly discussion. For your information and maybe to help you formulate better lies in future, no true daughter of Idemili could travel all that far into the bush for marriage sake. Where does she find her parents, brothers and sisters to discuss with? Whom does she run to when her husbands start maltreating her? Idigo, tell lies that are comparable to your age," his mother advised him.

"But she knows our father Okwundu, Ogbuefi Udemba, Arinze and even my father," Idigo refused to be cowed.

"Idigo leave lies so that lies will leave you," she shouted at the top of her voice.

"She even insisted that I should greet them," Idigo remained cool.

"Go and greet them now or have you done so already? But let me advise you, try and hide your faults a little, my son? Lies won't lead you anywere. It will only ridicule you in the eyes of people. It's a surprise that you took so great a pain to invent lies instead of agreeing with me that you don't know what I know; that garri destroys human sight. Idemili forbid evil."

"Who is arguingit?" a loud but elderly voice interrupted the one-sided match of words.

"Our father, it is your son whom you sent to college. He has refused to accept that there are things books don't teach," Idigo's mother said victoriously.

"My Son," Ogbuefi Udemba called out in fatherly tone, "these things are not in Oyibo books because they don't take garri. Whatever one doesn't know remain an enigma to one. What you don't know is older than you and deserves your awe. Never argue with your elders because time has been their teacher. What they see lying down, you cannot see even if you climb a ladder. Not even the ladder of academic education," he sermonised.

"And my bright child," she taunted him, "tell him who you said greeted him."

"Who is that?" Idigo's mother's lover asked to no one in particular.

"A daughter of Inwelle being married at Izombe," Idigo's mother informed him when no answer was forthcoming from a dispirited Idigo.

"Impossible!" pronounced Udemba with a wave of his hand after a short laugh. "Where is Izombe bye the way?" he asked after his judgement.

"In his School," she erroneously informed him.

The old man laughed once more.

"Even if all the money in this world are packed in that bush."

"She is married to a man there," she pursued.

"That is too much. Even if she is mad. No daughter of Idemili would go that far. Not even if all the men in this town are dead. No my son. Those areas are slave land where our people know very little about, seldom visit, let alone marry."

Idigo half listened to his uncle's misjudgement seething with anger and annoyance. Had she not mentioned his father and uncles by name, he would have thought likewise. But here was a good lady to whom they were well-known, asking him to greet them. And here was his uncle speaking like a man with a broken head dismissing his message with a wave of the hand. That made him a white liar and them, obvious intelligent wise victors. Intelligent they may be because there is no fixed fault-free index for measuring intelligence. But wise and victorious, they were not and he was poised to prove them wrong.

He threw his pair of slippers through the window. He then climbed through the window and went directly to Mazi Okwundu's house cursing his senior uncle all the way for his partiality and stupidity.

"My lion," Mazi Okwundu called him immediately he entered his sitting room. "Where are these children? Bring light here."

"I didn't even know you were in when I first entered. I was frightened out of my wits when you spoke," Idigo said after greeting his uncle.

"Many time, I prefer to sit down like this and think about the world," Mazi Okwundu informed him. "I learnt that you people of big book do it as well only that your thoughts only baffle me like someone telling me that the world is round and turning. Worst still that sometimes, we walk with our heads pointing downwards," he cleared his voice loudly. "Whoever said that should have his head examined, maybe he was thinking with his legs upside down. welcome."

"That is true. Most of them are really mad people," Idigo accepted so as not to alienate the confidence of his Junior Uncle.

"Thank you my son. You are thinking," he complimented to Idigo's joy. The uncle and nephew discussed extensively on a lot of issues and Idigo gave in to his uncle's arguments, theories, philosophies and the like just to win his favour.

"Are you well at all?" Mazi Okwundu asked when they brought the oil palm lamp.

"You look emaciated and frail."

"Yes, I am fine, it's just that I am missing school life," Idigo lied.

"You won't miss it long. You'll soon get used to it. You may even enter the big school. Try and keep your mind out of it," he was advised.

"Uncle, I just remembered that somebody asked me to greet you." Idigo started slowly.

"Who?"

"One lady at Izombe?" Idigo announced.

"Me? ' Mazi Okwundu asked in surprise.

"Yes and Ogbuefi Udembe, Arinze and my father."

"A woman at Izombe?" he asked as if he didn't hear well.

"Yes," came the monosyllabic answers.

"Who is she?" Okwundu asked as his thought scanned all possibilities.

"We call her Mama Elele."

"I don't know any Mama Elele," Mazi Okwundu announced innocently.

"But she knows you all. She said that she is a daughter of Idemili."

"I don't know of any daughter of Idemili at Izombe. That place is too far. What is she doing there?" he probed.

"She is married to a man there and makes 'elele' for us," Idigo answered though convinced that he had an uphill task.

"No, she cannot be a daughter of Idemili. No daughter of Idemili could be married in such far off lands," he announced politely.

"But she knows you all," Idigo baited him.

"Ehmm! I'm surprised but I don't seem to recollect. You would have asked her her name. But I am sure that no daughter of Idemili is married that far. Maybe she is from nearby villages."

"Yes, that is possible," Idigo conceded. "I assumed she should be from either Guru or Inwelle from the way she was asking of each one of you. She even reminded me twice not to forget greeting you people. I remember she said that we shall see again if I don't forget to greet you people," Idigo went on.

"That beats me then. I have always prided myself as knowing virtually all our daughters married away from home. I'll ask around to know if anyone could remember such a lady. Thank you for remembering. Though old-age might have caught up with me, I think I'm cocksure that no such daughter of Idemili exists. But I'll still ask," he promised.

They then discussed other trivialities, ate pounded cassava and egusi soup before Idigo eventually took leave of him much later.

Some of the children ran back to his door when he came back. They had peeped into his room after a long silence only to discover that he had disappeared. Idigo acknowledged their repeated greetings, shared the whole bean cakes among them and promptly went to bed. The children, ignorant of his disappointment and low spirits, wished all days be like that. That satisfaction, however, didn't prevent them from fighting over the plantain leaves used in wrapping the cakes.

Idigo didn't stop there, the following day he extended the message to Arinze who like his father was ignorant of the existence of anyone like Mama Elele. He, in the spirit of his father, was good enough to promise that he'll ask others.

Idigo, though visibly disappointed at the outcome of his moves so far, remained undaunted in his hope to prove that he took garri at school, that he did so with beans, akara or "elele", that the bean cakes were made by a woman married to an Izombe man, that this woman was a daughter of Idemili, that this daughter of Idemili knew his uncles very well, that this woman was supposed to be known to them, that this woman extended warm greeting to them which she insisted he should not forget to deliver and lastly, that he, though intelligent and learned, was not infected with the lying disease. He knew the weaknesses of his information but was not ignorant of its strong points. He vowed to prove his case beyond sane doubts even if it would entail going back to school to find out more from Mama Elele. But before then, he had to use the strong points to cover up the weak points. He wasn't very sure of the results of such an act but he was convinced that, at the worst he would generate genuine interest on the identity of Mama Elele.

After four days, Idigo went back to his uncle, Mazi Okwundu, when he didn't send for him (Idigo).

"My son, I'm sorry my enquiries didn't lead me anywhere," he complained. "Nobody seemed to know this woman that you are talking about."

"But she pressed so much that I greet you all and was so sure that immediately I do so, you'll know."

"Call me Arinze," Mazi Okwundu told no one in particular. "He said you told him as well and are convinced she could be known to us."

"Yes, she ought to be known to you all."

"I think so but really she is not," he confessed. "Arinze," he called when his son entered, "were you able to find out something?" he asked even before Arinze could sit down.

"No, father," Arinze answered as he sat down on the raised mud seat at one side of the room.

"Idigomgom, what does this woman look like?" he finally asked after a prolonged silence.

Idigo took pain to describe the tall, fair, beautiful, soft-spoken lady with a pointed nose and pointed canine tooth with a wide gap between her front pair of teeth. She has a prominent dark birth mark on one side of her mouth."

"Does she speak like our people?" Okwundu asked.

"Yes, except that it is frequently mixed with the Izombe dialect," Idigo answered.

There was a deadening silence for quite a period as each battled with his thoughts.

"And you said that she is married to an Izombe man?" Arinze asked.

"Yes," answered Idigo by then sure that the case was as good as lost, "but I don't know her husband in person."

"I was told that most of the people of Izombe are slaves or freed slaves. It is equally said that they are so mixed together that no one can easily know who is who. I can't see any daughter of Idemili marrying in that sort of place," Arinze solemnly announced.

"That is true," concurred his father.

"But she knew all of you very well," insisted Idigo.

"We shall enquire further." Arinze promised when he observed the disappointment in Idigo's eyes.

Idigo shrugged his shoulders in utter resignation.

"It is unfortunate that Chigbata is not around. I asked him to help in the enquiries. When he comes back, I'll know whether he found out anything. Presently, he went to consult an oracle because a very young royal python died in my yam barn."

"Maybe, the oracle wants to eat a chicken," Arinze joked.

"You young people never take things serious any longer. You don't take the warnings of the oracles very seriously thereby ignoring the revelations of disaster by our fore-fathers. That is the cause of the sudden increase in the rate of death of youths nowadays. The gods are annoyed with her youths. But no one cares any longer except we the elders. We shall do our best for all. Whatever we cannot do, we close our eyes to. Whoever we cannot protect, we let the devils take."

Idigo was visibly sad over the digression but he was aware that their investigations led nowhere and it was nobody's fault. Though he was satisfied with the effort so far, he promised to go on pressing his claims. Meanwhile, he was fed up with the old man's superstitious belief and could no longer restrain his opposition.

"And you believe in those things?" Idigo asked before realising it was rude of him to doubt his elder openly.

"What proof do we have for these things?" Arinze asked doubtfully.

Mazi Okwundu looked at his son sternly for sometime before he spoke.

"I can pardon this small boy," he said pointing at Idigo. "But your poor memory beats me hollow. You are looking for physical proof for spiritual things?" he asked. "Fortunately, they abound so you have forgotten Nnenna, my daughter married to that stupid Ogboli at Guru," he asked visibly annoyed. Idigo sat up when he heard that. Mama Elele was interested in that too. "And my brother Ngwu. . .," he stopped at mid-sentence as his eyes turned sharply to Idigo. He looked at the small boy for an eternity but didn't speak. Idigo was confused and shivered visibly wondering what had gone wrong.

"I'm sorry to interrupt you," Idigo apologised.

"No, what did you say now?" he asked soberly to Idigo's relief.

"She mentioned our in-laws at Guru," Idigo volunteered.

Tears ran down Arinze and Okwundu's faces as both bent down and pieced the puzzle together as easy as A B C. Mazi Okwundu was grateful that he didn't spill Ngwu's crime and his consequent awful death before his son when the emotion was too much for him. Idigo looked on as confused as ever as he looked from his uncle to his cousin. They were still in this pitiable condition when Chigbata entered.

"What did he say?" Okwundu asked without looking up.

Chigbata looked up at Idigo and back to his father. He would have preferred Idigo to go away but his father urged him on.

"He said that you denied her daughter. He said that the name of one of your sons is Egwuonwu and asked whether you are no more afraid of death. He said that another of your son answers Agubamba and asks whether you've found what you were looking for. He said that your only daughter is sad. That is all. I feel that this lady that Idigo is speaking about is Chinelo," he announced.

He got no reply because his feelings came some minutes late as the two grown ups there knew that just a shade of a second before he did.

* * * * * *

The meeting lasted far into the early hours of the morning. It would have ended earlier than that except that it was a family meeting. In addition, it wasn't an ordinary family meeting, but an emotional one. The emotions were mixed and each speaker had either expressed one part of the emotion or the other. The oldest members of the family expressed both because only few of them knew the sad side of the emotions. It happened right before their eyes though a long time off. They tried, however, successfully to play down this dirty part of their family's history. Generally, each speaker took an ample amount of time repeating the irrelevantly long and usually distorted story that have been heard time without number. But, thanks to good sense and judgement, none mentioned the culprit. Consequently, by the time they came to discuss the important aspect of their meeting, some of the people have stolen one or two 'tails' of sleep.

"But my people," Mazi Okwundu took over the initiative from a dosing Ogbuefi Udemba, "all these our joys and sadnesses are speculative. We are not sure that whom this our young lion, Idigomgom, the retriever of the lost, met is not another daughter of Idemili for, many were really kidnapped both before and after our daughter was."

"The description is unmistakable," Arinze cut in. "He said she is fair, tall, gap toothed, soft-spoken with a birth mark on one side of her nose. The last description told the whole story," Arinze concluded.

"That notwithstanding, we must confirm his findings and that is why I called all of you. We shall send some people to Izombe to go and identify her," Mazi Okwundu suggested.

"I volunteer to go but I'll need some other people to go with me," Arinze suggested.

"You still consider yourself a young man?" someone querried. "We still have young people in this family to do hard things for us. All we need are two strong people to go there, Arinze you won't go. I suggest that Egwuonwu, your son and Emegwo, my son should go."

"But they hardly know her. How can they identify her since they haven't seen her before," Arinze protested.

"Egwuonwu should know her," Chigbata said.

"I know Chinelo very well," Egwuonwu supported.

"He should know her with the eye of a kid. He may not be able to recognise her now," Arinze suggested.

"Even I and your father who knew her mother from birth may not be able to recognise her again. Twenty years is not twenty days; it didn't happen yesterday." Ogbuefi Udemba who had been asleep for the past ten minutes said.

"Anybody can go provided the person is strong enough to do the journey and fast too. We want people who can fight physically when the worse comes to the worst even though we aren't going to war. The question of identification does not arise. Our family mark is always our identity. Chinelo inherited it from her mother. Coupled with the prominent birth mark on one part of the nose, Chinelo will never be mistakable," Mazi Okwundu ruled.

The argument went on before Arinze and Emegwo, his nephew, were chosen.

"And remember," Okwundu advised, "your mission is very risky. But we are sending both of you because of its uttermost importance. You must both be careful so that we don't exchange one missing child for another. We shall count on your wisdom, Arinze and on Emegwo's strength of both body and mind."

"Remember that immediately you leave this Idemili land, everyone becomes your In-Law. For it is said that it is only by calling every stranger your in-law that one passes alien land; nobody is gifted to know all his in-laws both direct and remote," Udemba advised.

"You are not supposed to do any other thing than to identify her. Depending on the outcome, we shall see what we can do later," Mazi Okwundu reminded then.

"I thought we shall bring her along," Emegwo ventured.

"You must curb that tendency. If she is held as a slave, she must be sworn to an oath not to go home. So, until we are able to make them renounce the oath, there is nothing we can do. Just identify her, come back so that we work out a common strategy," Mazi Okwundu instructed, looked towards Ogbuefi Udemba who nodded his assent. "You must be really careful. Slavery has been prohibited but people still get kidnapped as if Oyibo people haven't arrived."

* * * * * *

Two men walked casually into the market place like every other trader. They kept as close together as possible with the younger slightly in front. They went directly to the place where butchers battled with flies, dogs and vultures for possession of their meat. There, they turned right as they were directed to where the vegetable and oil traders do more talking and gossiping than selling their wares. They turned right at the end of the row and looked each female trader strongly on the face from the beginning of the row to the end. Emegwo looked back at Arinze questioningly.

"She is not there," Arinze agreed.

"Whom do you want?" one of the women traders asked. "Come and buy my bean cake. It is very sweet. Look at it first," she begged as she unwrapped one for them. "Handsome man, how many will I put for you?" she persisted without giving them an opportunity to answer.

"We are looking for somebody, Mama Elele," Arinze informed her to her disappointment.

"I'll put enough 'jara' for you," the woman continued.

"I am her house maid," one young girl said, "she has gone down to the College to sell some of the bean cakes and to collect some debts the teachers and students owed her. But the cakes I have here are the same as the ones she took along. I'll tell her you called, "the young trader promised as she opened her basket and started putting some cakes into a piece of plantain leaf. "How many do I put for you?"

"Four", Arinze answered back involuntarily. "But we shall still like to see her." Arinze insisted.

"Are you people strangers?" the first woman asked as she detected the difference in dialect and had been looking the two men over and over since she failed in her attempt to secure a sell off.

"My In-Law, so you don't recognise me any longer?" Arinze asked in a surprised tone, or is it the quest for money that has confused you?"

"Oh, it is the trade, my in-law," the woman conceded. "This market is very rowdy today so that people don't recognise others very easily. Pardon me. How are your wife and children?" she asked as if she knew them.

"They are fine except for hunger," Arinze ventured as he backed out for the school.

"It is a universal problem that even the wizard Oyibos have not found a solution to. But you look so fresh and healthy to complain of hunger," she noted.

But Arinze and Emegwo half heard as they waved and edged themselves on to the road leading to Izombe College.

The two men followed the path Idigo had vigorously described to them back home. By the time they have made not less than twenty bends, greeting innumerable in-laws and rested to allow Emegwo eat two of the cakes, the School compound came into view, a bright star in this darkness called Izombe.

Arinze could not help being overwhelmed by the beauty of the college. He fed his eyes with the rolling grass lawns which descended to or ascended from the river depending on the way you look at it. He took a liking for the flower-lined walks, flower beds and wide fields lined with mango and other trees. The entire compound was surrounded by gullies which threatened its existence from all sides except from the river side. The compound looked near enough but they had to go down the hill, pass the river, climb another hill on which the School is precariously perched.

"Outside God, Oyibo people remain unchallenged," Emegwo summed up his observation.

"And hunger. They don't drink tea because they like it so much," Arinze corrected.

The two men continued that way until they sighted the erosion-threatened gate of the school. The cashew trees planted to check erosion hid the school compound from the road but the humming sound of the students was very distinct.

"Look at how these Oyibo wizards cut and tamed these hills," Emegwo pointed out.

"That is why we call them America wonder. Because they can do and undo anything," Arinze lectured.

"Except hunger," Emegwo pointed out.

"Except hunger," Arinze agreed. "And that is why we say that Oyibos are great but hunger is far greater than the Oyibos."

They kept on with their interesting discussion until they got by the School gate. The mini market was still in progress and students bubbling with the enthusiasm to go on holidays spent their left over cash on a variety of things. Some were busy mending their cloths, others their shoes. A significant majority fell over each other to buy bananas, oranges, fried groundnuts and say it; baked beans. Mama Elele was having some problems keeping the students satisfied.

Arinze and his companion edged themselves near the point of action but had to go back when they discovered that the students yielded no ground to anyone when the acquisition of this brand of bean cakes is involved. There was no respect for elders in Mama Elele's stand.

Arinze summed up the situation declined a suggestion by Emegwo that he forced his way through the teeming crowd thereby creating space for Arinze.

"We can't afford the luxury of bad publicity," Arinze counselled. "It was really crazy of us to get into that mad crowd. We shall be patient. After four days of journey, we shall not hasten into mistakes. Let's wait for this mad children to disperse."

He had barely finished when Chinelo announced that her cakes were finished. That did not keep the crowd calm until virtually each and every one of them had verified by seeing the empty basket.

The crowd had barely dispersed when Arinze and Emegwo had a glimpse of the woman they were looking for. Sure enough the birth mark was there but that wasn't conclusive.

Arinze went first but was closely followed by Emegwo.

"Woman, does it mean that none of it is remaining?" Arinze asked as casually as he could.

"Eh!" Chinelo exclaimed apologetically, "so, you people were waiting for bean cakes? It has just finished."

"Not even one," Arinze continued as his eyes moved over the unsuspecting lady from her mouth to her hands and back.

Chinelo noticed the scrutiny when she looked up as a result of the alien dialect and anxiety Arinze's voice betrayed.

"You people are travellers?" she asked.

Arinze found himself nodding with no definite reason.

"You are both tired. There are two remaining but I wonder whether it would do for you," she offered.

"It will," Arinze accepted while Emegwo watched on intently. Their eyes met and Arinze nodded. They were still speaking with their eyes when Chinelo tied the two remaining cakes and put it forward to them. They were still speaking with their eyes when she looked up in surprise.

Her eyes met that of Arinze and both pairs of eyes rivetted. Emegwo's eyes were rivetted to another part of her body; the hand with which she gave them the cakes. He was satisfied with what he saw, the sixth finger, their family mark. He raised up his two hands to show her his just as Arinze did the same.

The cakes fell back into the basket.

"Egwuonwu," she wrongly called.

"My daughter," Arinze responded.

Chinelo fell into Arinze's hands, tears ran freely down her cheeks, similar salty water soaked Arinze's eyes. Emegwo could hardly see with his eyes and desperate attempts to remove the big blocks ended up in producing more.

"It is all over," Arinze pronounced. "God is great."

"So Idigo is my son?" Chinelo asked between sobs. "Blood is thicker than water."

There were more sobs, the atmosphere became too emotional, people gathered and the mini-market came to a standstill which led to a premature dismissal.

* * * * * *

The news soon spread to the town and the big market was equally threatened with premature closure. But a big market was still a big market; it is seldom rocked to a standstill as easily as that. That, however, did not prevent a net exodus of people to late Mazi Alapa's compound. Where, an impromptu feast was in progress in reception of the two messengers from Inwelle.

Arinze and Emegwo never expected such a fanfare. They were supposed to be on a secret dubious mission. But here they were amidst a joyous crowd of both slaves and free-borns of Izombe, both sad and glad members of the Alapa family, both friends and enemies. Here were they among the liberal and conservative elements of the society, the sober and the drunk, the smiling and the weeping. Here were they where they wouldn't be, trusting whom they shouldn't, saying what they wouldn't, eating and drinking what they wouldn't; just doing the things they shouldn't do.

They hadn't planned things that way but emotions having ran high at the mini-market still held common sense captive at Mazi Alapa's house. First, Chinelo had led the way home and despite stiff protests from Arinze, they still found themselves following closely. They later wanted to leave that day for home, but Chinelo, her husband and others had refused and they had given in. The impromptu merry making, on its part, couldn't have been avoided.

At last, Arinze came back to his senses. "What on earth is wrong with us?" he asked himself. "Did they charm me? If it is charm, let Idemili forbid." He directly organised his thoughts and plans. He had been led so far and no more. He stamped his feet hard on the ground as if to show his last point of yield and his first line of counter attack. Beaconing his illegal in-law, he indicated his intention to address the crowd.

"I don't know how your people do but when we address a great people in my town, Inwelle, we do it with a great fanfare." Arinze parried his words.

"It's the same everywhere," some people urged him.

"My in-laws kwe nu," he hollered.

"Yaa," the excited crowd responded.

"The great people of Izombe kwe nu," he went on.

"Yaa," came a deafening response.

"Mighty Wamba people world-wide, kwezue nu," He pressed on.

"Yaa aa. . .," came a thunderously protracted reply.

He looked the silent crowd from left to right, from right to left and nodded mutely.

"My father used to tell me that whenever a great thing happens in a great man's house, in a great town, on a great market day, if a great masquerade is in attendance, it will receive great gifts. A great bright star has just sped across the dark night sky and I can see clearly now. I have always heard of the great Izombe people, how they taught the Oyibos some sense, their wealth and kindness. I had been skeptical but not any longer. The story told itself."

The ovation that interrupted him lasted for quite a period and gave him time to regroup.

"We came out in search of a badly maltreated, sickly, poor lady only to discover that our daughter was enjoying herself better than we do at home."

"And to worsen the situation, here we are being treated like Kings. We are not surprised at your reception because we were told but I have one request. Our people at home are too eager to drink the marriage wine from our in-law." The crowd cheered and the visitors were impressed. "We have seen she is happily married and we put our hand of support to it. She is happy here and that is the important thing to my people. We believe that whenever a child is, let him or her be healthy. We are happy with what we have seen and wouldn't wish it were better. By tomorrow morning, we shall be on our way so that our people would feel our happiness as well. I beg that you people continue to live in peace. I'll like to decline an offer that she go with us and see home before coming back. She has her trade to look after and her farm. When she finds time later, she could come. And remember, We'll like her to bring us news of when our in-law shall bring us the marriage wine."

The crowd laughed.

"These people and wine," one commented. "He keeps on hammering on it."

"There is no haste. We've lived without her for about twenty years. We can still wait a couple of native weeks. After all, a bachelor who insists that his relatives find him a wife sooner than later, with whom has he been living? Remember to give us about two or three months notice before you come so that we have time to prepare for you," he addressed his in-law directly. "We are not as rich as you people and so need a long notice so as not to disgrace ourselves. Our daughter is happy and healthy. Nothing is better than that. The road between our two people shall be like the way to the stream which never dries unlike the way to firewood forest which becomes lonely when the fire wood is exhausted. In fact, I've seen a couple of boneless girls one of whom may not escape us. Thank you all. Our people must hear of this reception." Arinze then shook a couple of hands and slowly sat down amidst wild cheers. He was glad with the effect of his message. It had worked like magic.

"I do not intend to consult anybody before I say what I intend to say," Chinelo's husband spoke. "My people feel the way I do. We are excitedly glad. Your daughter will pay you a visit three native weeks from today. All of us will then repeat two months later," he promised.

His people were surprised all the same for his unconstitutional pronouncements. No single individual has the right to fix a marriage date without due and prolonged consultation with others. But the atmosphere was charged with emotions and Chinelo's husband felt that the Inwelle people had been really kind in their offers. His response was the only easy way for him, to break the spell Idemili had on her which had made it impossible for Chinelo to have a baby. He needed a baby that resembled Chinelo very much and quickly too. Only a legal marriage could solve it. The sooner the better.

Arinze didn't object to the dates fixed. His body shook out of excitement over his easy coup. He patted Chinelo's hair periodically as he sat and listened. He had been doing so since they met at the mini-market. His hand was still on her head when the four of them slept on a pile of mats in their room. When he woke for the return journey early the next morning, her hand was still on his chest and his on her head. He loathed to rouse her from sleep but could not rise without doing so. She wept all the way as she and her husband escorted them on their way. He loathed parting with her at the River of the Seven spirits. All the way home, he could still hear her heart renting sobs. He and Emegwo moved like ghosts onwards and only her husband's parting words served as their solace.

"Till the next three native weeks as we said," he had said. "Safe journey. Greet my in-laws. Tell them we are well." And to his wife he said, "You'll soon be with them, cheer up. What of me that couldn't locate my people? I've even forgotten from where I came. Feel happy, not sad. A lot of people are looking at us. Wipe your eyes."

Chinelo had then obliged, wiped her eyes and they had gone in the opposite direction.

* * * * * *

The woman that the young men escorted into the compound looked beautiful in all shades of that word. All those who knew her mother had no difficulty in identifying her as Chinelo, the only daughter of Nnenna, the only daughter of Mazi Okwundu. She has come as was agreed at Izombe three native weeks previously The people of Izombe had kept their word. They had no alternative because the law was not in their favour neither were the gods. She wept as she walked slowly but steadily towards the compound's wooden gate. Her weary eyes scanned the area left, right and centre: a lot of things have changed since she left home. Big trees that stood as land marks had given way to new ones either voluntarily or by the activities of man. Formally unrecognised seedlings and shrubs had taken undue advantage of the absence of former large trees. Some thatched roofs had given way to metal roof and new houses had sprung up. The roads had changed direction slightly in obedience to the whims of overzealous farmers and new houses builders. She scanned the faces of anyone who fell into her hazy focus and recogrized a significant few. She would have done better if she hadn't been weeping.

The men that led her moved on solemnly at a pace dictated by her. They led her to the native doctor who sat majestically in front of the wooden gate. He had barely been introduced to her when he instantly proceeded in the process of spiritually reuniting her with her mother's family. He had barely finished by asking her to wine and dine without fear when the god of the land released the bounds around their emotion and shouted, "Go" All present, except the native doctor, who waited impatiently for his fee, wept like kids flogged by an elder.

Chinelo fell into the hands of his old and gaunt grandfather. "Father, Father, I've always feared I'll never set eyes on you again," she confessed.

"Idemili is still alive. I've always believed you were safe but recently, I started losing hopes of ever living to see you. My end is near. Speak nothing of this to anybody. Let them speculate. The Heavens

are greater than man. That is the name of one of my sons. Welcome."
The weeping then ceased except for occasional outbursts as new arrivals met her. The intensity depended on who came. But the sad memories that her return evoked soon found no room in the feasting atmosphere that soon followed. Goats, fowls, yams and cassava paid the price of her return or part of the price of those who sold her in the first place. The people who paid the other part of the later price were never mentioned. They remained at sea to many people except Chinelo herself, Mazi Okwundu, Arinze, Chigbata and maybe Idigo's mother. Even Idigo didn't know the part his father played. The name of Ngwu was never mentioned except once when Chinelo was weeping that her beloved uncle was no more. Nobody mentioned that early morning Ogbuefi Ngwu went to cut yam twine. Nobody mentioned that he mistakenly disturbed a bee hive. Nobody mentioned the agonising death. Nobody did. Chinelo took solace in Idigo whom she never left.

"I've always felt a strong attraction for this small boy," she once said later. "Ever since I set eyes on him five years ago, I've always thought he reminded me of a cherished one but I couldn't say who. I've always treated him as my own even to my own surprise. I never knew it was my brother I didn't recognise. Thank God I never denied him anything. I would have been accursed."

*   *   *   *   *   *

"Blood smells," Okwundu philosophised. "It is thicker than water. It was your blood that even pulled him to study at Izombe. It looks like resurrection. I wish death were like this so that lost ones reappear suddenly."

It was really like a dream come true for a lot of people. For days, friends and well-wishers poured in with presents. Chinelo visited a couple of places where she spent most of her time arguing with herself whether a particular feature was there when she left home. One of the places she went to was Guru where the reception was not less enthusiastic except that the only person she recognised faintly was her father's wife. Most of the rest, including her father, were no more.

She never slept at Guru. Most of her time were spent at Inwelle where the festive mood spilled over the entire period of two native weeks. Time flew past and the people of Inwelle took a lot of things for granted by the time she was supposed to go back.

Mazi Okwundu showed some alarm and surprise when she first mentioned it.

"You don't mean you intend going back?" he suggested.

"It was what the people of Izombe were meant to believe," she answered softly.

"Their belief could be wrong," Mazi Okwundu announced. "We didn't swear an oath to honour it because we are not legally bonded to them."

"But I can't stay without their leave," she pointed out.

Mazi Okwundu looked her seriously in the eye. Though he was encouraged by the fact that she had avoided referring to the Izombe's as her husband, he was chilled by the resolute conviction in her eyes and voice. He felt disappointed.

"You like them better than us, then?" he asked.

"Never. How can I? You don't understand," she complained.

"Understand that you prefer there to here?"

"No, not that. I am not free," she corrected.

"But we have concluded that already. The native doctor has eaten his own chicken."

"That is one part of it. But I was sworn to the Idol not to leave."

That was it. The information stunned all and sundry. Then Emegwo spoke.

"To which idol? To that piece of sticks, bird's feathers and bushes? That is no god. Our Idemili is much too powerful than that. Where was their idol when Idemili refused that her daughter would never give birth under bondage? Allow us to do our duty."

Chinelo thought over this for a very long time but said nothing. She saw great sense in what Emegwo said. Idemili had protected her.

"But she didn't prepare for this type of thing. She most probably left most of her personal effects there. So, she should be allowed to go. We shall, however, conclude a plan for us to come back to Izombe and fetch her out of that hole."

"She is not moving and inch," Mazi Okwundu suddenly affirmed. "They'll use her personal effects to do anything." Someone informed the audience.

"Father, they'll get me." Chinelo bemoaned. "Let me go and collect them. I'll surely return. I've been in hell over there. Please, let me go. Send people again to come and fetch me."

, Okwundu saw reason and by the early hours of the morning two days later Chinelo was led back home by one of her cousins. But not before hearing out plans on how they'll be coming back to salvage her finally for keeps.

* * * * * *

The two young men that casually strolled into Izombe market were just like the other traders to the casual observer. But anyone who took pains to look more carefully would have found out that they were fascinated by virtually everything they saw from the large market through the cheapness of things to the firm pointed breasts of semi-nude girls who went about unashamedly. Nobody in Izombe ever bothered to take but casual looks at others in market except he or she was looking out for somebody.

Chinelo stalked out her tendril-like neck frequently in search of people or things only known to her. She was very excited as she gave her numerous customers the amount of bean cakes each demanded but she frequently forgot to collect her money back. On several occasions, she had to be called back to her senses by good-natured customers who never took serious notice of this lapse. She had problems seeing through the crowd of people who milled around in no definite queue to buy her cakes. This made her nervous and unduly excited. She was, therefore, in a state of apprehensive hysteria when she spotted the two men in the crowd. She nearly shouted out of joy. That would have spoilt their well knit plan of her final rescue. In addi-, tion, their presence had brought her out of her dilemma of day-dreaming into the material realities of her escape bid. She had turned the scheme several times in her mind before this time. Surprisingly, the escape idea never sparked any enthusiasm into her spirits. The statistics of previous escape attempts were inconclusive owing to poor data; of all the numerous previous attempts, only two people's fate were known for certain. And both died in the attempt. The numerous others simply disappeared and no one could tell whether they made it or not. That dampened her spirits. But for one encouraging thing none was a proven daughter of Idemili, none was a confirmed child of this powerful god and therefore, not subject to her protection. That gave her hope. However despite this knowledge, she loathed tempting death because she wouldn't be opportuned to know if she had over-estimated the strength of her people's god, her intimacy with it , its ability in foreign lands and in the process ignored the sense of wisdom and reason by underating the not-so-powerless god of the Izombe people.

Despite this uncertainty, she had packed her personal things into a strong basket as she was directed. She made sure she never aroused any suspicion by complaining time without number that she was growing fatter ever since she returned from Inwelle. This was followed by intimation that she intended to mend all her dresses in the market to reflect this new development. Her husband was glad. A robust wife was a symbol of her husband's status. It indicated that she was happy which to many would only mean that her husband fed her well and took good care of her.

Chinelo's husband was unsuspecting when she asked her small maid to take the basket to the market for the subsequent mending of her cloths. He was rather glad before he left for the farms.

Chinelo's blood chilled at the sight of her brothers. That was the period of reckoning beyond which there was no turning back. She knew that immediately she left the market on any way not leading to her home, it ultimately would result in either freedom with its associated joys or to death and eternal uncertainties. She thought quickly by that split moment and decided that the risk was not worth taking. It was her contention that it was better alive and married to a slave whom she had no personal grudge against than to pursue a course whose probability of leading to death was not zero. All she needed to make her happiness complete was to have a child. And that was sure to follow when she had been formally married. No, she wouldn't go on with the escape plan. Everywhere is home where there is peace and happiness. No, having found her people, that was enough. By the way, what was she going to Inwelle to do? She was too old to get married again. Most of the people she knew were dead or about dying. It would take time to warm up with the younger ones. She would be odd in their midst. Besides, she was no daughter of Inwelle but of Guru where she was totally out of phase. No, she wasn't going, she would stay back and be legally married to this freed slave, raise children and die happily with the knowledge that she had relatives somewhere and that Idemili was always with her. She wouldn't feel lonely and lost any longer. She wouldn't feel astray and strange in the world away from them.

"Mama Elele," Egwuonwu called in a voice which didn't hide his excitement as much as it hid his foreign dialect,"are these the dresses you want us to mend for you?"

"Yes," Chinelo answered before she could restrain herself.

"Are they new tailors in this town?" a woman sitting near her asked when she couldn't place their faces.

"Yes, Madam," Egwuonwu answered, "and cheap too. We shall be coming back for your own when we must have finished all the work we have presently. They are very much."

"I have no cloths let alone one to mend. I grow neither fatter or slimmer," she confessed. "I equally have a needle and some thread for minor repairs."

Egwuonwu didn't wait to pressure the unwilling customer. He was already on his way with Chinelo's basket of cloths and jewelry on his head. Directly behind him and moving as fast as Egwuonwu was Agubamba who looked like Egwuonwu's apprentice.

They didn't carry their load to any sewing machine because there was none. It would be a surprise if anyone of them even knew how to pass threads into the eye of the needle of a sewing machine. Consequently, they didn't stop in the market or anywhere near it. On the contrary, immediately after jostling their way out of view from the market women staying around Chinelo, they changed course and headed for the main road leading away from Izombe.

Chinelo didn't know how she made the subsequent parts of her sales that day. Her blood was cold throughout but somehow, she managed to sell off her cakes and packed her basket. She had decided not to go ahead with the plan but hadn't resisted them from taking away her treasures. She had lacked the will power to resist and the one to go ahead. She was left between heaven and earth. She, was taken by surprise by the speed with which her basket left her side and had to look twice before she could convince herself that it was really gone.

"I can't leave all those things to go," she murmured to herself. "I wonder what I am afraid of. Afraid of man or god? Man can't do anything that god cannot. And Idemili is always there to take care of their god. I am going home," she vowed with the loss of all her cloths and jewels leading her thoughts along.

She beckoned her maid, gave her the empty basket of bean cakes to take home.

"I am going to see Ike's wife who gave birth last week," she said aloud for the other women to hear. "I have done her a lot of bad but I hope to stay long to compensate for going late. If my husband comes back tell him where I've gone to."

The maid nodded and went back home. Chinelo looked on as she left. She loved her maid. She was a nice girl.

"Prepare food and eat very well," she said after her.

Chinelo watched her disappear. She looked round the market with misty eyes and ghostly meandered her way to the outskirts of the market where she turned to a road much larger, busier and opposite to the one leading to Ike's house and the new born baby.

Chinelo went fast with her head bent and headtie brought low to cover part of her eyes. She looked suspiciously odd but many suspiciously odd things happen in the market and the roads leading to it. Within her, she felt mean to run away from her husband and other people. She looked inwardly dirty, and despite repeated attempts to justify her actions she ended up hating the idea. She felt cold inside and would have turned round and gone back. Yet, her legs moved faster forwards towards her cloth, jewels and freedom.

She eventually caught up with the two men later in the evening as they rested and waited for her under the Indian bamboo shade over hanging the road. By then, she had overcome her initial resentment and walked on more assuredly towards a permanent reunion with her blood relations. She looked forward to seeing her grandfather, uncles, cousins and Idigo in particular. But she felt inexplicably cold inside.

"I felt so cold inside that I don't know whether I am falling sick," she complained to her cousins after they had exchanged warm greetings not lacking in emotions. "My body keeps on shivering despite repeated assurances that I am doing the right thing."

"It could be the excitement of returning home finally that is overwhelming you," Egwuonwu suggested.

"Or the fact that you are making a change. It is not easy for someone to leave a place one has grown up in to love," Agubamba added. "When the body gets used to something, it resists changes."

"I think you are correct," she agreed more out of politeness than conviction.

It was getting dark and time was not on their side. A long stretch of trekking was still undone and they had to keep a comfortable distance between them and Izombe. They knew that Chinelo's absence would soon be obvious and a search would follow. They shrunk from the idea of the search leading to them. They had only one way of avoiding such an uncomfortable encounter and that was to keep moving and fast too. This they did, moving fast with Agubamba leading with the basket on his head and Egwuonwu taking behind with Chinelo. They did little talking, walked more and thought most.

* * * * * *

Chinelo's husband came back tired and spent. It had been one of those hectic periods in the farm when the work seemed not ready to wait and the muscles very eager to work. His muscles had always loved to work but the strains always told on it. Besides, old age was setting in and several muscles were rebelling. He felt so much pains from so many parts of his body that with time they became part of him. Only on certain rare occasions like when he bathed early each morning did he really feel that last year was not this year. Though, he was aware that the end was in sight, he never entertained any thought of giving up farming. And so, he had continued to suffer.

"Does it mean I shall not eat this night?" he asked as he pressed the bumps on his left leg where half a dozen blood vessels were attempting fruitlessly though vehemently to see the surface and maybe, take fresh air. "I have not seen smoke from the fire spot this evening," he observed.

"I have done the cooking long ago and I'm waiting for Mama to come back and put out the food," the maid meekly replied as she passed her hand over her stomach in acknowledgement that it had taken its full capacity of food.

"And where did she go?" he asked.

"She went to see Ike's wife who gave birth last week. She said Ike's wife would be annoyed with her for not coming early and as a result, she was going to stay long," the maid informed him.

"Let her sleep there if she likes but let her be kind enough to fill my empty stomach. Her visit to an old child cannot satisfy the thing I'm feeling in my stomach."

This observation of her absence was repeated several times before the poor man thought it was time to take a little positive action. Calling the maid, he assigned her an escort to visit Ike's house. This they did without much difficulties but the results weren't encouraging enough.

"They said they've never seen her there since they were blessed with a new member for their family," the maid had reported back.

"Eh!" asked the poor man in alarm and surprise. "But you said she told you she was going there."

"That was what she said," the maid confirmed.

Chinelo's husband went wild. His pains went instantly with the realisation that Chinelo was missing. The factor that drove away these pains also took care of his hunger and the worms it infuriated. In no time, the entire town was in their compound each person saying when and where she was seen last. Facts soon started falling in one by one and at long last the story looked fairly straight and clear enough; Chinelo was missing. A search revealed that she was nowhere around. Moreover, she hadn't collected her dresses she sent for mending. In addition, the tailors were strangers who lived only in the wind. Surprisingly, all her dresses required mending. Worse still, all her jewelry which required no mending by a tailor were equally missing. It fell in together to read in black and white that Chinelo had dared the gods to escape. People were disappointed, her husband felt cheated and the Izombe people felt it was a disgrace to their god and a reckless attempt to dare its abilities.

Immediately, the women were dispersed while the men sat down to plan a face save.

The meeting was brief. It was a direct challenge to their god which must be resisted by all means. Chinelo must be brought back by all means. She must be brought back dead or alive.

Every grown-up of Izombe was involved. The search parties included groups of men armed with guns, matchets, bows and arrows. Each group comprised between three and four men. They broke up at each junction so that a group took one road and another group the other. A group of rascal young men, fearing that Chinelo must have gone far, took a canoe to try an interception far down the river four villages away. In all, they were reminded then and again not to resort to violence unless her escorts chose such a line. Not mindful of any provocation, they would avoid any harm to their wife. This they carried like a live television show on their head as they went along.

The men on foot ran as fast as they could with the zeal of fanatical termites. Initially, they gained a lot of distance against Chinelo and her group. However, the energy of the body is not easily replenishable. So, with time, they felt tired and lost as much as they gained. No matter how much they tried, it soon dawned on them that Chinelo had gone beyond their reach. Each group either believed that Chinelo never left the town in the first place or that, if she had done so, not along the route they were assigned to search. In so many groups, arguments arose as to whether to continue or go back. The longer the arguments lasted, the greater the distance between them and Chinelo. By the following evening, the entire search party was in utter disarray while Chinelo and her cousins walked more peacefully home.

The three men in the canoe made the point where the road from Izombe and four other villages passed over the River of Seven Spirits via a mischievous pile of slippery stones and rotten tree trunks. By then, like the others, they had become tired more out of argument that the search was hopeless than out of the strains of paddling the canoe. Mosquitoes and tsetse flies had been unkind during the night and day respectively. The thought of taking back the canoe hadn't equally been very encouraging.

"I'll go back on foot," one of them informed the others.

"I've been mad to join this search so far. Thanks to the mosquitoes for their medicine. I have been cured. I won't go back this route," the other supported.

"I can't paddle this boat back alone," the third complained.

"Nobody asked you to," the second speaker corrected him.

"What do we do to it then when both of you have complained that you aren't going back with it?"

"We shall leave it here and do something with our lives," the first speaker said.

"No, I can't leave the canoe here. It is not fair on the owners," the third man sermonised.

"Saint Nweke," one of them called him, "why not take over the church from the Reverend father?"

"Leave the boat there, it doesn't belong to you. Nobody saw us take it so nobody will ask us," the other supported.

"It doesn't belong to me quite alright but I pity my uncle very much. He doesn't talk but by the way he'll behave like a wall gecko would make me pity him. I'll feel guilty. I'll rather suffer alone," he vowed.

The other men pitied him but refused to say whether they've changed their minds or not.

They felt so tired that they slept off under the big shade of the Indian bamboo trees that lined the river.

Nweke woke first. He thought he heard people speaking softly not far away. His body ached seriously as he propped himself up on his elbow to have a better view. His new view didn't get beyond the second bunch of bamboo trees. Consequently, he couldn't see the woman and two men resting by the road side, some bamboo trees off the road.

Chinelo and her two cousin had arrived a few minutes after the three men had fallen asleep under the shade of bamboo trees not far off from the road. The men would have seen them come down the road had they been awake. But having satified their curiosity that the road had they been awake. But having satisfied their curiosity that the sleep in turns until they were rested enough to go back by which way they may later choose. The power of nature had dictated the final action hence they all slept off.

"I'm totally fagged out," the female voice complained.

"Me too," one of the men agreed.

"Mine is unmentionable," the other man confessed.

"I can't resist the temptation to bath. I feel like soaking my body with cloths in this river for two days," Chinelo said.

The two men laughed and Nweke crawled closer to see better.

"I'll love to also," one of the men said and the other supported.

"Then go and bath. I'll wait for you here. When you finish call me and I'll come down and do mine. Don't stay long, we still have a long way to go," she reminded them.

The two men then stood up and went down to the river to bath. Nweke watched them closely but never knew anyone of them. That wasn't surprising because he was not supposed to know all the people in the four villages. But they seemed to have travelled far. They looked worn out like him and his group. But their dialect; it was just alien to the neighbouring villages. Nweke became suspicious and crept back.

He woke the two men who were too lost to the present world. He placed his finger on his mouth as each came to life. Both woke with mouths open suggesting each wanted to register an opposition to the unfair disturbance but for the finger on Nweke's mouth. They looked puzzled when he asked them to crowd their heads closer. They felt excited when he told them what he discovered. It was inconclusive but gave them hope at least. They were still deeply involved in their conference when a voice called out.

"You can come down now. We have finished," the male voice announced to more than one female.

The three men tensed and looked in the direction of the woman. Initially, they saw nothing and found it difficult to restrain themselves from going over to have a look at the woman.

The man over the other side repeated his message before Chinelo woke up with a start. She felt tired and rose with difficulty. The men saw her rise and couldn't believe their eyes. There was Chinelo in her beauty. They had become instant heroes in their town. They bent down just fast enough to avoid the suspicious quick glance in their direction.

"Let's take her now before she crosses the river to the men," one of the men suggested as he moved for action.

"No, she is not crossing the river yet. She is going to bath in it," Nweke corrected him.

"So, we take her in the river then," the man continued.

"It won't be as easy as that. We've forgotten our weapons in our canoe," Nweke the only sane fellow among them pointed out.

"She is no problem at all," one of the men said. "I can carry her on my head single-handedly to Izombe without batting an eye-lid," he boasted.

"And supposed she shouts?" Nweke asked furiously.

"One of you can close her mouth with his hand."

"But her brothers would be attracted by her first lone shout. And our weapons are not here. Even if they were here, Inwelle people are good warriors. The boys I see over there are also loaded with charms. It is even doubtful if a gun would be able to penetrate their skins," Nweke feared aloud.

"Then what do we do?" the other man asked. "Allow them to go just like that? No," he vowed.

"No, we won't allow them but let us work out a way of taking her without arousing the suspicion of her escorts."

The three men planned seriously for a time and at long last, they came up with a workable scheme which is though not fool proof.

* * * * * * *

One of the men crouched low to the other side of the road. He looked up and down the road and couldn't see the two men on the other side of the river. They had kept out of view to avoid seeing their cousin naked in the river. He innocently crossed the road to the other side. There, he found a convenient spot along which the river flowed, and got ready.

The best swimmer among them went in opposite direction on that side of the road. From there he could see Nweke making for the road. Immediately Nweke made for the road, the swimmer dived into the cold water and remained submerged.

Nweke made the road just as Chinelo had just finished bathing and made an attempt to come up the bank to dress.

"I am coming," she consoled her two escorts who waited out of view so as not to see certain parts of their cousin.

"We are waiting," they responded.

Then, she saw Nweke not very far off observing a group of weaver birds or one of the bamboo trees. He was backing her slightly so she couldn't see his face. She was sure he was a local indigene but that was not her immediate concern. More important to her was that the man, no matter who he was, was not going to see her naked; he wasn't going to see a single hair of her pubic region.

By reflex, she submerged into the river to hide her waist and chest region. The devil underneath had her . . .

* * * * * *

Chinelo struggled with whatever touched her legs but it was no use. She opened her mouth to shout to her cousins for help. She drank a mouthful of water, with her noise not heard anywhere except to the tiny fish which swam swiftly out of apparent danger.

Chinelo sank deeper and deeper inside the river with whatever was holding her not showing signs of releasing its grip. She kicked her two legs frantically for period and ended up getting tired faster. She tried to claw her assailant but discovered to her dismay that whatever it was, was pressed so tightly against her back that she couldn't reach it well with either of her hands. She tried to shout once more only to swallow another mouthful of water. She once got hold of a piece of stick but her joy was short-lived as the stick went down with her under the smallest tug. Hopes for survival got slimmer with time. She got hysterical and set on whatever it was with her teeth and felt its grip slacken. She felt tired but kept on biting whichever part of the assailant she could. The grip kept on slacking but she was at the point of giving up when she discovered the miracle, she wasn't sinking deeper into the river any longer but was eventually rising up. She moved fast and in no time, she was out and continued the serene and peaceful motion out of the water.

* * * * * *

Nweke and his town's man waited for their third brother to surface with Chinelo down the river as planned but to no avail. They walked up and down the river several times without any help. They came back to the pre-scheduled spot to discover, to their disappointment, that he hadn't surfaced.

"Maybe, he has surfaced lower down the river," Nweke suggested.

"And may have gone home with her to claim the honour alone," the other grumbled.

They came to the road, looked up and down saw nobody except the two young men with their basket of cloths and maybe jewellery. Strung on each's waist was a leather sheath on whose top showed the handle of a war matchet. They were looking for something.

* * * * * *

Egwuonwu and Agubamba had waited for more than forty minutes for their cousin to appear after her last call. But all in vain. Their annoyance gave way to alarm when their repeated calls yielded no response whatsoever. Agubamba had taken a careful peep in the direction of her cloths, and had found them intact. A similar one-eyed peep at where she is supposed to be bathing showed no sign of human life. He opened the other eye and tried the two together; the spot was deserted.

"She is no more there," he solemnly announced as he began to rise.

"Stay down, it is an abomination for us to see her naked," Egwuonwu informed him.

"If we see her naked, isn't it?" Agubamba asked, "let me see her first let alone that she is naked."

Before Egwuonwu could restrain him, he was off like a lion moving with swift legs down the river where Chinelo was supposed to be. Egwuonwu reluctantly joined him there. Together, they scanned both sides of the river on both sides of the road with no success. They were at panic point when they saw the two men.

The two pair of men, one armed, the other not, stared at each other suspiciously for quite a long time. Each was alien to the other. Egwuonwu couldn't contain his emotions.

"We are looking for the woman who owns those dresses over there," he informed the two worried and nervous men.

"No, we didn't see any woman at all," one answered with a shaking voice.

"You came down by this road?" he asked suspiciously.

"No, we are indigenes of this town," he answered quickly as Agubamba's hand tightened on the hold of his matchet. "We came out from this bush where we went to check our traps," Bishop Nweke lied for his dear life.

"Maybe she is toileting somewhere," the other man from Izombe suggested, "maybe, she has kept away because we are near her clothes."

There was some sense in what he said so the two groups moved away on opposite ways.

Egwuonwu and Agubamba waited unsuccessfully till late in the night before they decided it was safer and wiser for them to go home. They then left the River of Seven spirits like ghosts. They didn't speak to each other but moved like dumbs till they got to Inwelle.

They had been long awaited so, immediately their presence was made known, the entire village burst into life. All roads let to Okwundu's compound. But the people who saw them didn't see any woman with them. Some believed she was coming behind after seeing her basket of cloths.

One look at there faces, Arinze was alarmed.

"Where is Chinelo?" he asked.

Egwuonwu and Agubamba shook like leaves, waved their hands in resignation but said nothing.

"What happened?" Arinze shouted in fear and alarm as people rushed closer.

The story they narrated left both the audience and the lecturers baffled. Unfortunately, it led neither party nowhere near what really happened.

Their previous happiness turned out to be premature and instantly gave way to woe.

* * * * * *

The two men from Izombe met a search party looking for them at the outskirts of the town. They had been swearing curses to their missing member and each had been promising hell and brimstone for him whenever each sets eyes on him. The first question shook the hell out of them.

"Where is Ibe?" one voice asked.

"We thought he had gone home," Nweke replied in surprise.

"My people, listen to this type of nonsense," the leader lamented. "Three brothers went on a journey together and they have left their brother behind," he complained.

Nweke opened his mouth to tell his side of the story. But the time he ended, his audience all had their mouths open and agape but none said anything. The story left them more confused than enlightened.

"How do we explain this?" someone asked.

Nweke waved his hand in disgusted resignation. The search party went home demoralised, each member with his own opinion.

Nweke went home with his which wasn't definite.

"Maybe, he has eloped with the woman after sweeping her off her feet. It would be a strong temptation to resist," he had thought, "or maybe they had become entangled with one of the roots of the bamboo that lined the river." He shrank from the idea. "Or maybe, they had collided with one of the few stones that lie on the bottom of the river." That wasn't a palatable thought either.

Hence, by the time he made his home, he remained as mesmerised as he was at the River of Seven Spirits.

* * * * * *

Meanwhile, Chinelo kept on slowly but steadily on her solo journey home. She didn't know where she was going. She couldn't control her movements. Nobody was with her. Nobody directed her. She wasn't clothed because she had left her dress by the riverside and the rest were in the basket. But she never felt naked all the way in an effortless journey home. She felt no emotions except that of exhilaration as she did the long distance thoughtlessly but with great expectations. She felt neither happiness nor sadness though, if she had the choice, she would have preferred the former. She felt she was dreaming until she woke up.

* * * * * *

Chinwude waited for her husband to come in to her as he was opt to do for the period but he never did. She thought of going to remind him but that would have been unpopular; a woman begging her husband for company. She wasn't even expected to feel the urge let alone mention it. She walked past him repeatedly picking up little talks that were ignored because she was never seen nor heard. Satisfied that her scheme had failed, she settled for a long wait. She waited in vain. Sleep came naturally and stole her into oblivion. A painful pressure in her pubis awakened her and she had to do an unreferred race to the back of the house to drop her waste load. It was when she was coming back to the house that she, by then sober, observed that the door to their parlour was still open. She then peeped closely and saw a man sitting on the easy chair on one side of the door. She didn't look long to recognise her husband.

"He who takes most, suffers most," she said as she went forward to close the door.

"Leave it as you saw it," Egwuonwu directed from his reclining position.

"Let me close the door so that snakes and scorpions don't enter the house and kill my children," Chinwude pleaded.

"You are the first person I am seeing today. Don't bring me bad luck by disobeying or picking quarrels with me this early morning," Egwuonwu begged.

"So, you left this door to remain ajar throughout the night?" Egwuonwu said as he stood up and went into his room. "That is what is good for you, men," Chinwude observed. She then bared her tongue and pressed down her lower eye-lids with her hands. "You took your palm wine alone, it will deal with you alone."

Egwuonwu wasn't very glad with those comments but was sincerely in no combative mood. How he wished he had enough palm wine left in the keg to wash off all his sadness.

He groped in the darkness for the keg and soon found it. He shook it in one direction and then in another. There wasn't enough, but the remaining was manageable.

He took one cup, then one more cup, then one more cup then cups, then, the last cup half of which he couldn't drink because it was very thick dregs with impurities.

He belched loudly against a background of cocks crowing, dogs barking and the whining sound of mosquitoes.

"It happened a long time ago. I wonder why it should worry me now," Egwuonwu argued with himself. "Our people have changed a lot since then. Nobody can do those things nowadays," the alcohol in him said. "But worse things even happen in the world today and people seldom care," he managed to reason.

"What do I care," he finally said out aloud.

"You would care," Chinwude replied loudly. "Greedy man, you would care one day when you drown in alcohol," she continued ignorant of the fact that no one was quarrelling with her.

"I can now understand," Egwuonwu intoned. "A lot of people are usually forced to do things against their personal wishes. That is why worse things will continue to happen in a world which is getting more complex though it still has a long way to go."

He stood up and left the house to his wife's chagrin and disappointment.

"It is too early to quarrel," he said as he left for the farm.